Love Hurts
An Anthology

Edited by Eric M. Bosarge

Cover art by Diane Harrison
Cover Design by Leddy Creative Media

An
Eric's Hysterics
Publication

Copyright © 2013 Eric M. Bosarge

Published by Eric's Hysterics

www.erics-hysterics.com

ISBN: 0615759815

DEDICATION:

This book is dedicated to Megan, my rock, my love, my wife.
Anything is possible.

CONTENTS:

ACKNOWLEDGMENTS

I'd like to thank each and every one of the contributing authors for allowing me the honor of publishing their work. They are immensely talented, hardworking individuals, and it has been an absolute pleasure working with them.

I'd especially like to thank Wayne Scheer for continuously submitting to *Eric's Hysterics* and taking a chance on the publication in its infancy. It is always a pleasure reading his work.

Payne Ratner deserves special thanks for allowing me to include *Fish Story*, which was originally published in *The New Guard* and won the Machigonne Fiction Contest. I heard him read the story during my first semester in the Stonecoast MFA program and never forgot it. It is a fantastic addition to the anthology, and he was most gracious to let me feature it again here.

I've had the pleasure of working with Mike Heartz on several occasions and he was kind enough to allow me to use *Many Presents*, which was originally published in *OneTitle*. It is a great story which reveals some of the origins of our species' need for love and acceptance. I've no doubt Mike is a fantastic teacher and that he has a promising career as a writer ahead of him.

Without Michael Kimball this anthology and *Eric's Hysterics* never would have happened. He is one of the most generous teachers I have ever encountered; his contribution to this anthology is further proof of that. I simply cannot thank him enough.

Sean Leddy of Leddy Creative Media did an outstanding job on the cover design. It was easily the best Christmas present ever. I'm honored to have him as a brother.

And lastly, I'd like to thank my wife, Megan, for supporting me in every endeavor and humoring my constant questions and hounding for second opinions. She is my coeditor and first reader in every instance; a true a gift from God that I don't deserve.

HALLELUJAH
by William Klein

Robert was pretty sure that every time people prayed the rosary they were actually thinking about fucking. He was perched on a pew in the back of a chapel that exemplified our Lord Jesus Christ's love of varnished pine and stained glass. To his right was the reason Robert was thinking about fucking. She was also the reason he was praying the rosary, even though Mass—which they had also attended—ended a while ago and this was some sort of extra innings bullshit that no one knew Catholics actually did.

Minnie was radiant. Her blond hair fell in loose curls under her black sunhat, across her plump neck, and about her sleeveless cream dress. The dress was trimmed with black silk that matched her hat; double-breasted with metallic buttons that glittered in the stained glass light. It did an amazing job of displaying her tits. A wide, black belt covered her stomach. Straight-backed, her hands clasped the rosary at chin level; the strength of the prayer caused her breasts to jiggle slightly. Unlike Robert, mumbling the Lord's Prayer with the rest of the meager congregation, Minnie clearly enunciated every syllable.

Her poise faltered when she noticed Robert's gaze. Squirming on the hardwood, she chewed her red lip before picking up at the next Hail Mary.

Robert's weekends were for reading fine literature in his lawn chair and sipping bourbon as early as he could. The Lord had no part in that and He knew it. He tried to stay out of the King of King's business, and trusted the King did the same. Robert hoped He wouldn't mind their covenant being broken. Minnie had started going to church and, if that wasn't bad enough, she insisted on bringing Robert with her. As a man moving comfortably through his mid-thirties, Robert reasoned that crises of the spirit were his domain and it was rude for someone in their mid-twenties like Minnie to overstep their bounds like this.

Minnie arranged the rosary in her lap. She sidled towards Robert, her soft hips and cushiony bare arm pressing him. In the multi-hued patchwork of light he picked out the fine hairs on her shoulder, her neck vibrating with prayer.

Minnie placed her left hand on Robert's knee. Still praying, it began to trace spirals up his thigh. Robert, who kept mumbling with the best of them, attempted to shift away. Minnie's hand clamped onto his groin like an iron pincer.

Robert ceased mumbling, moving no more than if he had awoken to find a panther on his bed. With her right hand, Minnie fingered the next decade of beads. Her left, which seemed to be not so much unaware of what the right was doing as just not giving a fuck, hooked his waistband. She slid onto the kneeler in front of them, dragging Robert down next to her.

For once, the controlling force in Robert's pants was not his penis and he was pulled into a half respectful kneeling posture. The congregation droned on. He gave Minnie a bewildered look. *What the fuck was going on?*

"Pray," she hissed. Minnie's sinning left hand untucked his shirt. *Good Lord, I hope she doesn't decide to cut it off,* Robert thought, approaching a sincere prayer. Under the tent of his shirt and somewhat sheltered by their bodies, Minnie unzipped Robert's dress pants. Voice steady, she reached in and gave a small gasp of pleasure. Another decade passed while Minnie was content to let her hand rest. Robert's knees ached. Then, concluding the Paternoster, but before the next Ave Maria, she began to stroke.

She did not go fast at first, but as they moved to the Antiphon she gained speed and vigor. Robert, for his part, spread both elbows on the pew, gripping the rosary with white knuckles, head bent in the picture of holy contemplation. Sweat pooled on his forehead, his nose slicked enough for his gold wire spectacles to slide down the brim. During the

Apostle's Creed, Minnie lost the ability to contain minute whimpers. Robert gritted his teeth and concentrated on his breathing. They made it through the last three Hail Mary's, picked up speed during the complementary Our Father, and climaxed during Hail Holy Queen. A long *ahhhh* escaped Minnie's lips when she felt his release, smiling wide as she remained bent over her rosary. She wiped off on the inside of his shirt and allowed him to tuck and button.

"Go, in the name of the lord," said the priest. The crowd mumbled a repeated reply.

"Hallelujah, hallelujah!" called the priest.

"Hallelujah, hallelujah," the kneeling figures replied.

Robert remained beside Minnie as the congregation rose and shuffled out.

An old couple exited the front pews. The man shakily genuflected at the aisle; his wife helping him up. How many children had they had? All properly baptized, Robert was sure. What had their bodies meant to each other once? What did they mean now?

An Irish-looking family was leaving, a gaggle of dark-eyed children being shepherded by their parents. They had thin, drawn mouths. Did they still greet each other once a month in the marital bed, on the proper cycles prescribed by the Pope?

Behind the altar stood the priest, a wrinkled man with an indistinct halo of gray hair. How much had he given, or given up on? Was it a price he paid knowingly every day, or a debt that accumulated without much thought? And what about the mournful figure that hung over his shoulder?

A stained glass depiction of The Virgin Mary loomed over him, the blue and red of her robe blazing and the glass of her halo glowing with love. As a life-long virgin who had a husband to take care of, she at least would have approved.

* * *

When they arrived home Robert went straight into their bedroom to change his pants. In fresh briefs, he sat on the bed. *What the fucking fuck?* Like any red-blooded American, Robert had no problem with a handy J in church. He thought it would make a fine tradition, keep the heart in shape—much like the Swedes running into the snow after a sauna. But Minnie had never done anything like this before. Their love life had always been perfectly satisfactory.

Two things Robert feared were change and the unknown and he was extremely cautious about letting them into his life—even if they came with hand jobs.

He went into the kitchen, where Minnie leaned across the bar counter. Sunday sun splashed her face and down her neck and chest. Smiling dreamily, Minnie pushed a glass of bourbon across the counter. The ice sparkled the smile of an old friend.

"Ah, thanks?" Robert said, wondering what he was referring to. Alarms were going off; Minnie never made him drinks. She had a glass of wine some nights, but deplored liquor.

"I'm meeting up with Mandy and the girls." Minnie was part of a pack of other accountants from her job. Robert had vague notions about what they did; sit in cafés and drink frou-frou coffee drinks, scour farmers' markets for organic produce, or hold appetizer potlucks and drink wine. These activities usually dominated the weekends. Once Robert had been a regular presence, dragged along like a sullen toddler and left to play with the other boyfriends, with whom he shared little other than a dejected air and a penchant for putting alcohol into things people did not expect to contain alcohol. However, that had been some time ago, and Minnie was content to leave him to his weekend sessions of drinking cocktails, reading, and falling asleep in the afternoon sun.

"I've got to get changed. See you this evening?" Minnie trailed her fingers across his chest on her way to the bedroom.

"Mmn," Robert grunted, trying the bourbon with trepidation. The bedroom door drifted open. Her full frame slid out of the dress, revealing the lingerie—all silk lace, ribbons, garters and hose. Robert had not been aware that she owned any such garment. She undid the clasp to free her large breasts, reaching towards one of the sturdy cotton bras that

Robert was more accustomed to seeing. Robert took a long drink.

Robert was a man of routine, and after The God of Abraham's meddling this morning, was eager to return to it. He had attended the finest State College a middle-class income could afford, and had broadcasted the fact that he considered himself an intellectual with his choice in bourbon. Four years later, he'd been handed a degree in business and took the first job offered in a town where no one could dispute his intellectual superiority. He kept to himself, growing his intellect with an even more intellectual brand of bourbon and reading leather-bound books that he occasionally enjoyed. Those who did get to know him liked his dry humor and sharp wit, and wondered why he didn't make more of an effort to socialize. If anyone had ever challenged his quiet, bespectacled dignity by asking him he would have tried to articulate the comfort he felt from simply existing. But it probably would have come across as an excuse for being too lazy to stop being lonely.

What Minnie loved about Robert was that she was the one area of life where he tried. Though Robert regarded things that did not come easily to him as a waste of time, something about Minnie was an exception. Robert was a drifter by nature, and accommodating a woman as feminine as Minnie required unrivaled effort on his part.

A year ago, Minnie's great aunt Ethel had passed. This

was a shock to Minnie. Until she pulled the surprise move of dying, her great aunt had inhabited the background of her mind; an institution of childhood that continued perpetually without involvement, like Sesame Street. They had prayed the rosary at the service, and it had brought back the religion of her girlhood. The bowed wooden faces of the saints peering down at her, the cryptic intonations in Latin, the sternness of the pews, it was mystic and ethereal and fulfilling and Minnie felt herself enlightened by something she had been missing. She felt herself offered a promise of something larger. But each time she went back on her own she felt the promise less clearly; the worn velvet of her too comfortable life wrapping itself back around her. She wanted the promise to be a part of her, she wanted it to take her sepia existence and make it something miraculous. Robert would never come willingly, but the priest assured her that salvation was hard and she knew this to be true.

* * *

As the week went by and the holy hand job settled comfortably into the past, Robert began to relax. It became a memory in which Robert's hunched and mumbling figure was a lightning rod that Minnie resisted for as long as possible, but gave into with quivering loins and hands. Robert was relaying these sentiments to his only work friend Leonard on a slow

Friday afternoon.

They were in Robert's office; Robert leaning back in his chair, Leonard on the edge of the desk. Robert had just finished telling the story to an amazed Leonard.

Leonard was small with thin, blond hair and a mustache that wanted to be big and strong when it grew up. The newest member of the firm, he was still young—not yet thirty. Robert had taken Leonard under his wing, not just as a senior fellow employee, but as an older man. However, the real reason Robert enjoyed talking to him was because Leonard was a miserable little misanthrope who would never invite himself into Robert's life.

"Wow," Leonard said. "Right there in the church?"

"Oh yeah." Robert reclined further in his chair, attempting to put one leg on the desk but misjudging the distance and almost upsetting his trash can.

"Why would she do that, do you think? Is she into shit like that, or what?"

"I don't know, sometimes women just get into weird moods." Robert was reluctant to think about it—the idea that something unknown to him lurked in Minnie's sexuality.

"Did she do stuff like this when you first met?"

"No way, never. I guess you weren't here when we met. After Minnie got hired at our accountant's she started coming around every once in a while to drop off papers and stuff. I could never get a chance to talk to her, so I started losing things. You know, those reports we get from them and the analyses they do, stuff like that, hoping they'd send her over. It worked for a while, and I would make conversation, but I couldn't be losing things constantly. Then one time after I 'lost' something instead of Minnie they sent an electronic copy. They had finally gotten an internal network running in their office. So I snuck out, walked over to their firm, found her desk, and handed Minnie the folder I was supposed to not have. 'I lost this,' I said, and told her not to bother looking for a replacement. I was pretty sure they were out, but I knew there were spares at the diner across the street if she was free for lunch. Couple years ago, now." Robert leaned back, enjoying the memory of surprise on Minnie's face, followed by the flush of pleasure as she agreed.

"Reminiscing on old times?" Minnie said from the doorway.

"Hey, honey…bunches," Robert struggled for an appropriate endearment in his surprise. He resisted finishing with 'of oats'.

"Hello to you, too. Dork." Minnie tossed a folder onto his desk. "Just came by to bring you this. I'm on the move this afternoon, but I wanted to see you."

"Oh yeah? What's got you so busy?" Robert flipped the folder open to reveal a fairly standard tax breakdown of his investment figures. His office still kept master copies, and he got files like this about once a month.

"I wanted to drop off some dry cleaning, and it's got to be this afternoon if we want to wear it Sunday."

"Sunday?"

"Of course. Church, silly."

"Oh yeah. Duh. Church." Robert looked up from the folder. Was her smile just a little salacious? As she leaned in did her hand linger on his knee a little longer, move a little higher on his leg? Her lips seemed to linger on his cheek for longer than a good-bye peck warranted, and he lost his train of thought for a moment.

"See you at home?" Minnie asked.

"Yes'm," Robert said, dazed. He fumbled her hand as she left.

Leonard remained, arms crossed, looking put out.

"What?" Robert asked him.

"This is bad news, dude. You guys never used to go to church, right?"

"She's into it lately. I would rather not, but she really wants me to for some reason."

"And she gets all randy while you're there?"

"Just that one time."

"Just that one time, so far. I know women. When they change like that, it's for a reason. She wants something. And not your Johnson in church."

"Leonard, you have never known anything, about any women, ever. And as for what women who become sexually aroused in church want, I am the sole pioneer in an exploratory field, and I say it's too early to draw conclusions."

"Alright man, but I'm telling you, there's more going on here. This isn't going to be one hand job. This is, like, a whole mountain of hand jobs worth of trouble."

"Get out of my office. I need to be alone while I figure out what a mountain of hand jobs would look like."

"If you say so, but you'll see."

During the rest of the afternoon, Robert had a hard time getting work done. Minnie didn't want anything—everyone got horny sometimes. She just wanted to mess around. He would see next Sunday.

* * *

He did see next Sunday. And the Sunday after that. And the following Sunday. It never got as bad as the initial hand job in the pews, but Robert couldn't fully enjoy himself. He managed to shuffle Minnie into a unisex bathroom or out into the car, but each time was a closer call as Minnie became more demanding and passionate earlier in the service. Then there were the new outfits and lingerie bought for Sunday use. They had the money, but why?

None of this prepared Robert for what came next. As they walked into the narthex through large wooden doors the change in Minnie was noticeable. She stiffened, took his hand firmly with one of hers and laid the other on the inside of his bicep. *Oh God, and we just got here.*

Robert was wearing a freshly dry-cleaned suit and tie that hadn't seen use since he and Minnie went on actual dates. Minnie wore a new sleeveless lavender stretch satin dress.

As the priest introduced the Mass with personal tidbits and bad jokes, Minnie's intensity receded. She used a softer touch, sinking against Robert's shoulder in a way that she had not for a long time. Robert remembered how it had been for the first couple years of their courtship. They had always touched each other, just a hand across the shoulders, or knee, the other acting as anchor for the way life moved around them. Whenever they waited somewhere, in line at the bank or to cross a busy street, Minnie had hooked a finger into Robert's pants pocket. What had changed? Certainly they did not love each other any less, but Robert could not deny it was different. After moving into their house they had run together, like rain drops on a window. Now they rarely touched because there was no part of their lives that didn't touch already.

The Mass passed smoothly, except for Robert's unsuccessful attempts to will away an erection. The memory of previous Sunday's exhibitions combined with Minnie's close proximity proved too powerful. *Great,* Robert thought. *I am now at the point where being in church gives me a boner.* When communion rolled around Robert made the mistake of rising slowly, attempting to conceal his arousal. Minnie, who had sprung to her feet like a game show contestant, hooked his shoulder and dragged him upwards.

Two slow lines moved down the nave for wafers of Eucharist from the priest, before moving to receive the blood from golden chalices proffered by dour-faced elderly women. As Robert limped along, he noted Minnie's hands clasped in front of her breasts, chewing her lower lip as she fretted her way down the line. When it was her turn to receive the body of Christ she lingered an extra moment—eyes closed in rapture as the wafer dissolved on her tongue.

Son of a bitch, Robert thought as he eyed a similar wafer being placed in his hands. He had resolved to shove his piece of Jesus' body into his mouth when Minnie, who had just wiped excess wine from her lips and sucked it off her finger, captured his hand and dragged him from the altar.

When they entered the deserted narthex Robert dug in his heels.

"Where are we going?" He tried to pry his hand from Minnie's, who'd gained Samson-like strength. Minnie whirled and pushed him against a wall. Hands entwined in his jacket lapels, she slid a knee across his hips, her mouth close to his.

"There's no talking in church." Her breath was hot and he smelled her perfume. Her cheeks were flushed and her eyes looked glassy.

She tried the unisex bathrooms, but both were locked. Minnie whimpered. She spun Robert, pushed him the way they had come, dragged him back across the narthex, which now held one or two elderly devotees holding stacks of pamphlets by the doors, awaiting the conclusion of Mass. Robert had learned the Mass schedule in the previous weeks, mostly for the purpose of scheduling hand jobs. Communion was one of the very last things on the holy itinerary. He could hear the priest dismissing the congregation; soon people would flood from the narthex and into every corner of the building.

Minnie pounced upon a stairway, dragging Robert down it. In the basement they found a cafeteria with several doors. Robert could hear the rumble of feet on the ceiling, combined with the murmur of voices. Minnie chose a door and pushed him through.

The lights were off; shafts of sunlight came through small windows near the ceiling. The air was cold and crisp from a window someone had left open. Robert caught his breath; the sound of birdsong coupled with cars on the street, as well as feet coming down the stairs. There were several rows of desks that were too small for an adult. Pasted on the concrete walls were cartoon bible characters drawn in plump outlines with name tags: Noah and his ark, Abraham, his wives and the un-sacrificed Isaac, Samson, arm in arm with Delilah, Lot with arms around his two daughters, Judah and Onan with Tamar between them.

In a sunbeam from a window was the teacher's desk. It

held charming little wooden blocks that displayed the date, a set of plastic trays filled with papers, a coffee mug full of writing utensils, bible-themed coloring books, and various other educational debris that Robert suspected was about to become a jumble on the carpet.

Sure enough, Minnie forced him onto the desk, and Robert felt like a prophet as it all went scattering to the floor. She opened his fly while hiking her lavender dress up to her hips. In what must have been the cafeteria's kitchen, pots and pans scraped.

"Are you not wearing any-Mph!" Robert was cut off. Minnie had wound his tie around her hand and yanked his mouth to hers while she straddled him on the desk. Her free hand arranged their particulars and having them so arranged began to grind against him.

"Oh my God," Robert groaned, placing his hands under her ass. Minnie slapped him across the face.

"This is church! Mnh! You do not! Uhh! Take the Lord's! Ahh! Name! Ohh! In! Yeah! Vain! Oh my God!" Minnie put his tie between her teeth. The desk shook from the rocking motion.

Minnie came out of the classroom first, followed closely by Robert. They stood in the cafeteria, not looking at each other. No one else was around. Robert adjusted his tie, while Minnie straightened her hair. *Jesus Christ, what the fuck?* Robert thought in something probably too profane to be a valid prayer. He heard the steady hum of voices from above.

Minnie gave him that dreamy smile and walked slowly up the stairs. Robert followed, still struggling to fix his tie.

Mass had let out and the church crowd had their mingle turned up to eleven. At the top of the stairs Minnie turned to him with wide eyes.

"Oh, golly! I forgot I need to go check the bulletin board!" She dashed off, quickly lost amongst the confusion. *Golly?*

Leonard appeared at his elbow.

"It happened again, didn't it?"

"Leonard! What are you doing here?" Leonard wasn't religious. Robert looked him over, attempting to comprehend his presence. He wore a light baby blue button down with a cornflower tie and navy Dockers.

Realization dawned. "Oh my God, have you been following us here?"

Leonard grinned.

"Do you think that church people can't see blue or something?"

"It did happen! Why is one side of your face red? I knew it would! I just knew that little minx couldn't resist getting all lubed up for Jehovah! Look man, you got trouble."

"That little what? Lube—"

"Robert, you're missing the point! Minnie's going crazy on you, man! She's turning into a full on slut for God! How are you going to deal with this?"

"A slu-"

"I'll tell you what you need to do, what you need to do is cut her loose! Don't you see? She'll want it in crazier places and crazier positions! How long do you think you can keep that up without getting caught? How long do you think you can keep it up at all? Look man, the point is, this is the fucking point, the point is that she's not working her loins into a froth for you! She's found religion and now she's hot for the Son! Of God!"

"Fro—"

"Oh shit, here she comes!"

The crowd parted to admit Minnie, holding several folded papers in her hands. "Hello, Leonard. I didn't know you were a church going man."

"I try not to make a thing of it," Leonard replied coolly. Then, much too loudly, "I don't go balls out like some people!"

There was silence. Robert looked at Minnie with pleading desperation, who looked at Leonard like he had a growth on his face, who looked at Robert with a hopeful grin, who looked at Leonard like he was a child who had put his finger in an electrical socket, who looked at Minnie like he thought the full heft of his joke might sink in any moment, who was looking at Robert as though he had just invited that friend no one likes to a night out.

"Hey, Minnie!" Robert said, finding his voice. "Would you get the car? Leonard and I need to talk about a work thing for a minute."

"Sure. Okay." She left, clutching her papers.

"Balls out?" Robert hissed. "That doesn't even make sense–you addressed it to her! Leonard, seriously, what are you doing here?"

"You need someone watching out for you, man. This is bad news. Bad news McGruze. This is just where it starts; God only knows where it will end. You need to get out man, fast. I gotta go, my great aunt goes here and I'll never get home if she sees me."

"Leonard—"

"Watch your ass, man." Leonard produced a pair of mirrored aviator sunglasses from his chest pocket. Combined with his mustache he looked like a poster warning children about talking to strangers. Leonard followed the stragglers out. He looked back for a moment and Robert thought he winked, but couldn't be sure because of the glasses. Other than a statue of Jesus extending his hands towards him, Robert was the only one left in the church.

* * *

The next week was a bad week, and it only got worse as Sunday drew nearer. The papers that Minnie had come away with weren't announcements, they were activities. Church activities. And Minnie had been making a schedule.

Monday: Jesus quilts for the homeless and the most compulsory blowjob Robert had ever been party to. He had been reading on the couch and hadn't been given much choice in the matter, considering that his book had been thrown across the room—and not by him.

Tuesday: Soup kitchen at the local Y and Minnie joining Robert in the shower. Robert had been afraid to under-perform lest Minnie take matters into her own hands and they slip on the porcelain. He was sure the neighbors heard them, or at least her.

Wednesday: Redecorating the Sunday School classrooms (along with gossip about the raccoon that had gotten in and messed up the teacher's desk) and Minnie—who knew Robert was only pretending to be asleep—vigorously riding him reverse cow-girl until he sat up and put his hands around her breasts the way she liked.

Thursday: Community Potluck organized by the Knights of Columbus and a session of cunnilingus that made Robert feel like he had stuck his head in a bear trap. At least it didn't exacerbate his chafing. Minnie had arrived home late, and Robert had contrived to be in the back yard, ostensibly stargazing. When he heard Minnie coming around back he had been in the front, checking the porch's molding. When she came around one side he had been on the other, inspecting the gutter—couldn't be too careful now that winter had passed. However, Minnie knew that Robert had to sleep sometime, and so had been waiting for him in bed in nothing but a slip with candles lit.

Friday: A poorly attended "Teen Alternate Night" and the realization that, even in public, Robert was not safe. He stayed at work, and afterwards went to a café several blocks from home, eating organic cold sandwiches for dinner and drinking wine with a shaky hand. Somehow she knew. Robert took a long drink of wine as Minnie sat down at his table. When he ignored the various and increasingly obvious hints that she wanted to go home, she reached out and pushed his wineglass into his lap.

"Oops." Minnie batted her lashes. "We had better get you home and get those clothes off."

Afterwards, while Minnie was curled up against his chest and Robert was stretching out thigh cramps, Minnie dropped the bomb on him. Tomorrow there was a church picnic at a nearby lake. Minnie, of course, had helped organize it. And he was going.

Minnie slipped off the bed and walked to the closet, doing a full-body stretch that involved going up on her toes. Robert could not help but admire the way her breasts defied gravity. She was picking out clothes for him to wear tomorrow.

"I'm going to be up and gone early to help get things

ready, but I expect to see you there around nine?"

Robert, whose body was retreating into sleep as a desperate act of self-preservation, started.

"Hey, honey?"

"Mmm?"

"Maybe I could just skip tomorrow? I'm pretty tired, I could really use the rest."

"Skip?" She turned from the closet, smile growing on her face. Minnie walked to the foot of the bed. "But Robbie, I need you." She had a pout in her voice that he knew well. The blankets were yanked off and she crawled up the bed towards him. "Robbie," she moaned, kissing from his knee across his inner thigh. When she spoke he could see white teeth behind red lips. "How can I do this without you?"

* * *

The next morning was such a perfect example of spring that it seemed designed to taunt Robert. A good thunderhead with thick, anti-picnic rain and he would have sung hosannas. He stood in front of the open refrigerator in his boxers, chewing his way through a package of bologna. He knew there would be food at the picnic but he was so hungry. Dark bags sagged under his gold wire glasses. When an alarm clock he was sure he had unplugged woke him, he found clothes laid out. Underneath the clothes was a pair of dress shoes that Minnie loved but he had always hated, along with folded socks. *At least I get to decide which boxers I wear,* Robert thought, wondering if he had any that locked. He couldn't take this anymore. He finally had to admit that he had no idea what was going on with Minnie, but he might not survive much more of it.

Robert pulled into the lake parking lot at nine-fifteen a.m., the exact time Minnie's note had indicated. Something about finding the note on his clothes, and then on his wallet, and then on his car keys, and then on his dashboard had made him afraid.

He was locking his car door when he heard a voice behind him.

"Robert." Robert's head sank against the window.

"Oh my God, Leonard."

"Robert, look at you man. Jesus."

"Leonard, I didn't get much sleep last night, are you really there? I'm not looking."

"No shit you didn't sleep last night, look at you! Robert, I've been watching you. You look rough. You're shaky and irritable, and whenever someone closes a door too loud you have a mini freak out! Is it this church thing? Is she making you pound her at church? What's going on with this church thing?"

"Leonard! Why do you even care? I swear to Christ, if I turn around and you're wearing all blu—oh my God, you are! Why is this any of your damn business?" Still famished, Robert set out for the picnic at a brisk stride. Down the shore he could see colorful tents, tables with food, and people gathered around them.

"Why are you walking like that? Is it because of her? Did she give you something? Like, church herpes or something? Okay, don't look at me like that, not church herpes then. But still, man, you can't deny that this is some bad scoobies. Why is she doing this? Why does she want you sexing her all the time like this? Does she want to get hitched? Is she baby crazy? Does she want you to put a little Jesus baby in her? But you're not married! Doesn't that mean that like, Jesus won't love it or something? Look, you need to cut her loose. Make her weird, disgusting church fetish some other guy's problem, you know?"

"Leonard—"

"Oh look, cupcakes! Look man, I'll stick around, fly reconnaissance, you know? Make sure everything's on the up and up."

"What? No, Leonard—"

"See you soon." Leonard strode away, navy clad legs pumping towards the cupcake table. As he receded Robert saw him fish in his front pocket for his aviators.

He couldn't worry about that now. Where was Minnie? Still hungry, he eyed the food. He wasn't as young or fit as he used to be, and strenuous exercise on a full stomach would be uncomfortable.

When he didn't find her at the first tent, he was agitated. When she wasn't at any of the tents he became nervous. When he didn't find her at the volleyball court, the horseshoe pit, the donations table, the barbecues, or the picnic tables, he approached panic. He turned in circles, trying to be aware of what was going on behind him. Everyone had seen her, but no one knew where she was.

He was on the trail through the woods to the outhouses, checking them as a last resort, when a pair of hands covered his eyes. Robert began to sweat.

"Hey Robbie," she cooed. "All alone?"

"J-just looking for you, actually." He began to grow hard. *Traitor!* The movement was painful on the raw areas he had been developing all week.

"Well, isn't that a coincidence." Minnie's voice was dangerously soft. "Me too." She removed her hands from his eyes and stepped into view. She wore a sun skirt that fell to her knees with a dark cardigan over a jogging tank top that pushed her breasts out. Her golden hair shone against the green of the forest, and it fell in a loose pony-tail over one shoulder. He steeled himself.

"Look, Minnie. We got to—"

"Get to the outhouses? Why Robbie, you dirty boy. At a church picnic, too. C'mon!"

"The outhouses? Are you fucking—Minnie. Minnie!

MINNIE!" She stopped.

"Robbie?" She'd made it several feet down the trail before realizing he wasn't following. "Robbie, what's wrong?"

"Minnie, what the hell? What's the deal with you lately?"

"I don't know what you mean." She looked confused. The flush Robert had noticed was fading.

"Are you serious? First you start going to church, then you start making me go; now you're jumping me every time we're in church or there's some church thing going on!"

"No, I just, I thought you would like it."

"I did like it, at first! But I also like resting, and not chafing! And, and I just need to know what the deal is. You apparently get hot for Jesus like you never did for me. Is what we had not good enough?"

"Good enough?" She didn't look confused anymore. "Good enough? What we had? What do we have, Robbie? What do we do? We go to work, and then we come home, and that's it! You spend your time reading 'fine literature' and drinking gross old-man bourbon and I know exactly how much. We don't even talk about work because, let's face it, our jobs are boring as hell. We've lived together for four years, and where is it going? What's changing? You do the same things over and over, you act like you're better than everyone else when you're really too afraid to even find out, you can never find anything to say that doesn't sound good as a sarcastic quip, and you care about your own life so little I wonder how you can care about me! Our life fucking suffocates me. I found something at church, and don't you dare laugh at me. It made things better, for a while. Then worse. I guess it made me stir-crazy."

"Yeah, no shit!"

"Robert, don't—"

"Min, I can't do this. I can't keep up with you, and if this is the kind of person church is making you then I'm not sure I want to."

"I'm serious, Robert. I need more."

"I understand Minnie, but I'm not sure this is a life with room for me in it." After a moment of internal struggle, Robert walked away.

On his way back to the car, Leonard emerged from a bush.

"You've got to be kidding me, Leonard."

"So, are you guys going to bang, or what?"

"God. I'm not asking. No, Leonard, we're not going to bang. I need to sleep on your couch."

Leonard considered this until they arrived in the parking lot. Robert could see himself doubled in Leonard's glasses as Leonard placed a hand on his shoulder.

"Okay, Robert. But I have to warn you, as a respectable person I'm going to have to make a rule about religious activities in the house."

* * *

Leonard's house was everything Robert had hoped it would be, which only made him sadder because Minnie had loved making fun of Leonard with him. Now he would never get to tell her. Flanking Leonard's Xbox in the living room was "the triumvirate": Life size statues of Xena, Hercules, and the Highlander. Robert sat on the couch, staring at them morosely. *His own pantheon of saints.* Leonard brought him a beer.

Robert was hurt. When had he become not good enough? Eventually he went home to get clothes, things. Only when he knew Minnie would not be there. The first time he had spent a half hour sitting on her side of the bed. What surprised him most was that his existence was not fundamentally changed. He had his books, he reallocated his bourbon supply, he went to work, and he was unquestionably Leonard's intellectual superior, if not his equal at Halo.

He moved out, found an apartment. He already had everything he needed, and lacked the impetus to drift home, so it made sense.

Then Robert did something that surprised him. He went to church. He wished he knew why so he could denounce it as a stupid reason, but he didn't. He certainly wasn't any more of a believer, he felt no balm on his soul, and once he got over the Pavlovian expectation of being jerked off, he became bored. But he went, and on some level it comforted him. Robert kept going, enjoying the play of the stained glass light over his skin, and the sternness of the varnished pine pew beneath him. He always sat in back, but started getting smiles and nods—at first only from the priest, then from the elderly, and then from the rest of the congregation, pear-shaped women and thick-necked men stuffed into bright shirts, but it was nice to think that somewhere, someone considered him a good person, even if all he did was show up. Something about that made him realize that he had more to give, and gave him faith that it would be worth it. He sat in his back pew studying his own sinning hands; it wasn't long before their match showed up.

DOORWAYS
by Jamie Mason

Ever since the accident Corrine had problems with doorways. Some girls had problems with organizational skills or menstruation or their emotional lives; Corrine dematerialized in a fine quantum spray of atoms and reassembled elsewhere each time she stepped through a doorway. She could never predict where. This was the price she paid for having a theoretical physicist for a father, and playing too close to the quantum destabilizer with her Barbies when she was a kid.

Boyfriends never stuck around long.

Robert was a jock—captain of the boys' hockey team. To his credit, he would risk the social stigma of dating a geek girl because he prized intelligence. Once he accepted her habit of climbing through windows to enter and exit buildings, they had a lovely autumn romance. They took long walks, shared secrets and traded books. Robert said his favorite novel was The Bell Jar. "It's so sad," he whispered, tears in his eyes. Corrine decided he was a keeper. Hockey season came and he started inviting her to games. She demurred upon learning the arena had no ground-floor windows. When he threatened to leave her if she missed the finals, she promised to come. On game day, she glimpsed him waving excitedly to her from the turnstiles. She took a deep breath, entered the building and rematerialized on a construction site in Beijing. He stopped returning her calls.

In desperation she began dating Zach, president of the Physics club. She knew she was just playing out her daddy issues but Zach's understanding of general relativity gave him a real shot at appreciating her problem. But Corrine found it surprisingly difficult to be frank with him. She kept talking around her dilemma, hoping to buy time. Meanwhile, Zach was pestering her to come see his positronic isolation chamber. Corrine pacified him with laudatory texts in response to the photos he e-mailed her. But when he lowered the boom and demanded she enter the lab with him or else, she broke it off. Memories of Robert's ultimatum were too fresh and besides—plane fare home from overseas was a bitch.

She could never make it to parties, so people just stopped inviting her. The remainder of high school passed in a cloud of isolation. She spent prom night alone in her room, surfing the Web and guzzling Diet Pepsi. At some point she switched to gin and, in a moment of drunken depression, walked directly into the kitchen. She rematerialized in Pittsburgh and had to hitch-hike home. A trucker named Dave was sympathetic.

"I didn't go to my prom, neither," he admitted and gave Corrine a Three Musketeers from his stash of candy bars.

College presented major problems. Corrine didn't even want to imagine what switching buildings for each class might do to her. So she decided an online education was the solution. And she found a one-room apartment on the ground floor of an apartment building near the train station. Things were looking up.

She graduated with an IT degree and found a good job to which she could telecommute. She made oodles of money so having groceries delivered was no problem. The only hassle was loneliness. She climbed out her window one afternoon and bought a kitten from a pet store down the block. She named it Albert (after Einstein—who else?) and spoiled him rotten. Because he was a cat and attuned to quantum nuances, he taunted her by continually stealing her wireless mouse and running into the bathroom with it to see if she'd follow. Once, distracted during a conference call, Corrine did just that and rematerialized, Albert in hand and the wireless phone receiver sandwiched between her shoulder and ear blaring a disconnect signal, outside a U2 concert in Los Angeles. She hiked to the highway and stuck out her thumb. A familiar truck pulled over.

"Pets're a hassle," Dave admitted. "But it sure beats bein' alone. Wanna Mars bar?" He treated Albert to some ham from a truck-stop sandwich.

Corinne teleconferenced in for her next Monday morning staff meeting and saw a stranger sitting at her boss's desk.

"Marjorie's on maternity leave," the stranger announced gleefully. Corinne experienced a sinking feeling in her chest but soldiered through the meeting, contributing the bare minimum to demonstrate she was paying attention.

The baby-boom spread like a plague. Corrine's job security grew as her coworkers migrated to split-shifts, half-time, quarter-time to accommodate emerging domestic realities. She scheduled a day off when Marjorie invited her to participate in the baby shower via Skype.

"Oh, this is wonderful," Marjorie gushed, voice squeezed fuzzy across the connection as she un-wrapped the jammy set Corrine had Fed-Exed. "Corrine you're going to make an amazing mother. When are you planning to have yours?"

Corrine tried not to feel jealous. But she logged off a half-hour later and got smashed on Chardonnay. In her tipsy upset, she almost followed Albert outdoors but stopped herself in time. Blinking back tears, she fired up her PC and tried to work. But it was pointless. She finished the wine and stepped through her front door, not caring where she ended up. It turned out to be a beach in a rainstorm. She sat in one of the changing rooms and cried until dawn. Then, barefoot and drenched, she climbed up the path to the highway. A woman bicyclist stopped and asked what was wrong.

"I'm just so lonely," Corrine sniffed. "I'm turning thirty in a month and I have no man, no family. I wish I could have a baby so I wouldn't have to keep ending up alone when I go through these doorways. But it's never going to happen."

The woman in the helmet and track suit told her to hang in there, patted Corrine's arm and pedaled away.

Corrine pondered her child-birth options. There was always artificial insemination. Or she could just go to a bar and pick up a stranger. But the complications would come after—not before—the act of conception. She shuddered, imagining them trying to wheel her into the delivery room. What if she ended up in labor on the other side of the world? She had been lucky this time; the license plates on the cars said Florida. What if she ended up in Siberia? The best she could hope for would be someplace like Canada that had socialized medicine, but luck had never been her strong suit.

A truck pulled over. The passenger door opened.

"Long time no see. I been thinkin' about you," Dave said.

"I'm miserable," Corrine confessed. "I'm so lonely. I don't know what to do."

"Marry me."

The abruptness of his proposal surprised her. Haltingly, Corrine explained her problem with doorways. It was a long drive and Dave listened sympathetically. When she was done, he said he still wanted to marry her.

"You mean it?" For the first time in years, she was hopeful.

Dave laughed. "Why not? Listen, you think you got problems with not being there for people? Try bein' a trucker."

Corrine said she could sympathize.

"I run through Vegas this trip." Dave glanced at her. "I know a nice little place we can get hitched. We can tie the knot, then go play some slots. It'll be fun!"

She smiled. "You won't mind if I keep disappearing through doorways?"

Dave shook his head. "We all go through 'em alone. Important thing is to have someone waitin' on the other side when we get there. That's my job. Now stop crying and have a Hershey bar."

I'LL LOVE YOU FOREVER, BUT…
by April Grey

You know, it was a marriage they said would never last.

Even I had my doubts. After all, I was a dancer—a dancer, mind you, not a stripper—at the Pussy Cat A-Go-Go Club and he was this geeky post doc at his friend's bachelor party. But I became a good professor's wife. I hosted faculty teas and luncheons, kept the house spotless, made healthy meals, kept myself in shape and raised two beautiful boys—one now at MIT and the other at Cal Tech.

Still, it's supposed to be until death do you part. Death: the parting of the ways. This whole eternity thing, I never agreed to it.

Faithful to a fault, that's my Fred.

And he wasn't buried three days when he showed up at the back door covered in dirt, and his feet, well, he had no shoes on, just socks. Wet, muddy, slimy socks! He should have told me, put it in his will or something, to bury him in shoes. I would have done it. I can be unconventional. He should have warned me, but he was always the typical absent-minded professor.

I was in such shock that I hadn't the presence of mind to shut the door on him, and then he was on my freshly washed kitchen floor, with moldering leaves and what have you, and he grunted at me.

"Huh?" I said, equally speechless. I kept that floor clean enough to eat off of and now look what he'd done.

He grunted again. Prior to his demise, my Fred was a well-spoken man, and he had this amazingly plummy voice for his lectures.

"Fred, honey, I don't know what you're saying."

He opened his mouth a bit wider and a few white crawly things, slugs, maggots, I don't know, fell out onto the floor. I shrieked and ran for the disinfectant and my cleaning gloves. While I was under the sink, trying to decide on straight ammonia or pine fresh, he shambled over. He tried to embrace me as I stood up with my supplies. Well, no way, I thought, though I was pinned to the sink. He smelled of soil and decaying things.

Still, I tried to stifle my revulsion. This, after all, was the father of my boys, so I didn't want to hurt his feelings. Neither could I accept letting him get one inch closer. I put out both my hands, filled as they were with cleaning products.

He grunted plaintively, perhaps at the expression on my face, and turned around, moving toward the living room— oh, my white shag rug! The one that I waited years for the boys to grow old enough to head off to college before getting. The one that I made everyone take off their shoes before walking on. That one!

Well, yes, Fred wasn't wearing any shoes, but that only made things worse; there was already a trail of grime across my kitchen floor. I know Martha Stewart claims she can get out dirt from shag, but can you take the word of a jail bird?

It was time to lay down some guidelines.

"Fred, Lovey," I said as I got out some chilled wine from the fridge. I froze. I had had that wine in the fridge chilling since before his accident at the lab. The dinner I had planned that tragic night was trout almandine with green beans and rice. Healthy meals, that's what I strived for. Pulling myself together, I found the corkscrew and opened the wine. "Please sit down and have a little. I know this has been a stressful time for us both. Why, the boys lost a week from their classes, and only flew back last night. I'm sorry you missed them."

I must have been getting through to him because he turned away from my shag and came back towards the kitchen nook where I had poured us two glasses of wine. I patted the wrought iron café chair, hoping he'd take a seat. I only meant to sip my glass of wine, but the sight of him and his yellowing, hard boiled eyes, upset me. I downed it and poured a second.

"Sweety-kins," I began, using the back of my hand to wipe away a dribble of wine from my chin. "This isn't going to work out. You know I adore you, and I'll love you always."

He moaned and the sound of it drove a cold chill down my spine. I forgot what I was going to say for a moment, while I wondered what that green and fuzzy thing was on the side of his nose. Was it growing there?

He was trying to say something, maybe that he loved me too. But did he love me enough to stop this insanity and head back to his grave?

"You know, you can't stay here. You're dead and your new home is in the cemetery. Remember? We picked out the grave site together. You really loved those cypress trees!" I tried to be as gentle as possible. "And the funeral, I guess you don't remember that, but the boys were there and all your colleagues from the University. And what would they all say after such a beautiful ceremony? It would be downright rude not to stay dead." I gulped down another glass of wine and felt the room whirl.

"And I promise to visit you every week. Won't that be grand?"

He didn't touch the wine, but grunting even louder returned to the entrance of the living room and my shag rug. I hadn't gotten through to him at all, and now my rug was about to pay the price! Where was that reasonable man I had married? Gone forever, I feared.

I didn't know how I would stop him but I ran past him into the living room and stood in front of him, wordlessly begging him to stop. But stop he didn't. Instead, he pushed past me and crossed my rug leaving a dank, black, oozing trail across it. But the rug was not his final destination, and he entered his study. I was tempted to shut the door behind him and lock it. Then what would I do? I had to somehow get him to understand his place in the world was the graveyard now that he was dearly departed.

Inside the study I found him tearing through his desk. He slipped a vial of some grey-green concoction into his coat pocket, and then continued to throw papers on the floor. His study was the one place in the house where I wasn't allowed to go while he was alive. After his demise, it had taken me hours to collect and sort his papers, but I didn't complain about this new mess. I can be noble.

With a happy grunt, he found his research journal. It was his habit to have two sets of notes, one in his study for him to pore over at night and the second one at his lab. I smiled and nodded—maybe he just wanted some reading to take with him?

He brandished it at me. I read the cover, "Immortality Project." I sighed. Poor, poor Fred. I usually spent the time when he was talking about his work figuring out the dinner rotation or the week's grocery shopping in my head. Had I known, I would have told him what a dumb idea it was.

Immortality? Who would fund something like that?

"Is that it, Fred? You wanted to tell me what you had been working on? Well, I understand. It all went wrong, horribly wrong. You're dead now, and it's time to head back to Shady Elms. I'll miss you, but I'll come by every week with fresh flowers. You'll see that being dead isn't too bad."

With a howl he rushed forward and lifted me up in his arms. I shrieked, and then I kicked and pushed against him, but to no avail—he was walking on my beautiful shag again—this time headed for our bedroom. Now I didn't have just one filthy path to clean but two. I had to admire his strength though; lugging me around like that should have thrown out his back, but here he was carrying me without a moan or even a grunt.

I've always been careful with my husband's feelings. Scientists are like artists, sensitive, but he just wasn't getting the message. Something dropped off of him and wiggled itself down into the shag. I screamed and pounded my fists on his all too solid back, enraged that not only would I have to get it cleaned but fumigated as well.

But just when you'd think it can't get worse, it did. He crossed the threshold of our bedroom and I realized that he was about to violate the pristine ambiance of our bedroom.

"Put me down, Fred. I'm not going to make love to

you. No, means no!" He ignored me. Crossing the pale pink and beige carpet of our bedroom, he tossed me on the bed like a sack of turnips.

"Please, in the name of all that is holy, there are 400 thread count Egyptian cotton sheets on this bed."

Sex, great sex, had been the mortar of our marriage. In the bedroom, we were frenzied, exotic animals pounding out our differences, but I draw the line at necrophilia.

I opened my mouth to tell him no one last time, but he grabbed my jaw. With surprising deftness, he un-stoppered the vial I had seen him put into his pocket, and poured the stuff down my throat.

It was as if liquid nitrogen had been poured into me, instantly freezing my mouth, jaw and neck. It slid down my throat into my stomach, and an intense iciness enveloped my torso and spread through my limbs.

The only heat remaining was my tears pouring down the sides of my face.

As my vision faded, Fred leaned over and mouthed some words. I can't be sure, I can only hope, but I think he said, "Trust me."

Well, maybe Martha was right about getting dirt out of shag...

MANY PRESENTS
by Mike Heartz

"Matt—what are you doing? It's me."

"Nothing—just sitting here not working."

"How's the hand?" He was off work for a week after he
shattered his hand punching an unread *'Leadership in Business'*
book on his desk instead of the petrified underling who stood
before him. He failed to see the irony.

"Fine. It hurts. The Disney Channel is running a 'Family
Matters' marathon."

"Nice. I need you to get out your old Santa outfit—go to
the store and buy two video games and bring it to my class
and give it to a kid named Vincent."

"Not a chance."

"Or I'll tell your wife that you pissed yourself on purpose
when you were driving home drunk from the bar after work."

"Go ahead. That was years ago. She wouldn't care."

"Wasn't that the weekend you got out of going to her
parents for her aunt's funeral because you said you thought
you had ulcers?" Never was I happier that my best friend, in

addition to having a short fuse (it was the third time he had broken that hand angrily punching inanimate objects) was also a budding hypochondriac.

"What time?"

It was Valentines Day, always in the running for the worst day of the school year. Halloween was a close second. Whichever one I woke up to is the worst. In the minutes after a Valentine's Day class party, it's not unusual to see elementary teachers knee deep, reeling in a pinkish heap, covered in unyielding glitter and cupcake residue on the tiled floors gasping for spring.

Immediately after Martin Luther King Day, the students' minds are swimming in pinks and reds as they dreamily backstroke in a heart-shaped pool of cheap chocolate, miniature candy hearts adorned with generic expressions of love, and cherubic bow and arrow-wielding baby angels. The only impediment to their enthusiasm is an annoying thing called school.

And of course, the classroom party is the coup de grace.

The teachers are merely lifeguards of the day. We understand the ceremony of it all, but most of us are hardened to the bullshit holiday and forget what it means to the kids: free candy, declarations of "like" for classmates, the subsequent denials of "like" when everyone knows they *do* like them, and the passing out of non-gender specific "friend" cards with a side of fairly predictable art projects. And everything is festooned in hearts; little ones, big ones, paper ones, all different colors, shapes and sizes. It doesn't matter. All that matters is that it's something resembling a heart.

For weeks leading up to the big day—along with many notes home, I had to explain, and remind everyone that if they didn't bring in a card for everyone, then they will not be able to pass out their cards and treats. No one's getting the shaft at my Valentine's Day party. Just giggles and sugar rushes—and possibly a few eternal love matches. All it takes is someone not to get their cheap, generic Incredible Hulk card—that didn't even have their name on it—and the slighted will break down like someone just beat their kitten. Cards for all—or none at all. I'd be supplying the pizza, so that somehow hid anyone who didn't bring in cards. Pizza is always the main attraction and distraction.

I was surprised I made it fifteen minutes without anyone asking me about the party but wasn't surprised by the inquisitor.

"Mr. Thomas?"

"Hand." Willy could not remember—but I wasn't giving in to him. It was a yearlong war.

"Yes, Willy? And remember…"

Like a tight-noosed prisoner with fifteen seconds to say an hour's worth of last thoughts he spat out, "Can I pass my cards out now just in case I get sick or my mom comes to get me early or we forget to have the party or you have to leave or the principal cancels school or something else bad happens?"

I did admire his tenacity—but not when he was trying to usurp my authority. "Willy—its 8:15. I'm a little surprised you even have to ask that question—*not really*—but I *am* a little annoyed by it. As I've said all week—we will have all the Valentine's Day hoopla at the *end of the day*—the last hour or so. Please—no more questions about it—I know you are all excited, but contrary to what you may think, this *is* a regular school day and we have a lot to do until we get to any party. Yes, Antonio?"

"South America."

"What?"

"What country I think we are."

"No. I said, 'contrary to what you may think'. Not 'country'. It means, 'against what you may think'. And South America? That's a continent, my friend. We're the United States of America, remember? Now get back to your morning work. We have a lot to do."

That was a lie. These days were never normal—I knew that. I just tried to get through the day. I planned on loading them up with enough Valentine's Day busywork to get them to lunch and then a quick Social Studies lesson to bridge the gap until the festivities kicked in.

At 8:20, Victor walked in with a late slip—sobbing.

"Big V—what's wrong?"

"S…San…Santa not coming today!" he stammered before exploding in tears.

"What did you say, Victor? Just try and relax and breathe." I really didn't know if I heard him right. I couldn't have.

"Santa Claus isn't not gonna come today." Despite his double negative, I knew what he meant. His mucous was flowing freely now and I couldn't help but think this could be bad for the rest of us if he ever let the stuff solidify. One half of the Booger Bandits was going to be fully loaded for the holiday. Antonio had to be jealous—this kind of production was a goddamn goldmine. A good cry could restock a booger arsenal for a full day—no self-inflicted blows to the nose for him.

"No. You're right buddy. Santa is *not* coming today. Why did you think he would be coming today? It's not Christmas. We just had Christmas a little over a month ago."

Settling his sobs down to mere whimpers he hiccupped, "My dad kept saying Santa Valentine was coming. But when I woke up this morning—there was no presents under the tree. It was just the cat under there."

"You guys still have your Christmas tree up?" This was the ultimate sin in my book. Christmas trees come down on January first or earlier.

"Yes. But there were no presents and my dad was

sleeping. He kept telling me to leave him alone when I tried to wake him and ask why Santa didn't come."

"But Vincent—*why* did you think Santa was coming?"

"Cuz my dad kept saying Santa Valentine's Day was this week. I thought he was coming back. He's dressed in red like all the hearts and stuff. And he didn't give me many presents but two video games at Christmas and one of them broke the first day. So I thought he was coming back to give me the rest of my presents. My dad kept saying Santa Valentine's day was this week. But he not coming!"

"I'm sorry. You're right, Vincent. He's not coming today. He's not coming until next Christmas."

I knew his dad spoke limited English so I took a stab and called our foreign language teacher who teaches Spanish and German.

"Laurie, how do you say 'Saint Valentine's Day' in Spanish?"

"dia de san valentino—no capitals," she sing-songed perfectly.

"Alright, thanks—I think I figured it out. Vincent is down here balling because he thought Santa was coming today because his dad was telling him it's 'dia de san valentine' and I think all he heard was 'Santa Valentines Day'."

"Ooooh. Yeah. If English is the dad's second language, Vincent might have heard 'Santa'. But it's *Valentine's Day!*"

"Yeah—well you and I know that. Big V thought the jolly old fat man was coming for round two and gonna leave him some *working* presents this time. Thanks. I gotta figure something out. Talk to you later."

Turning from the phone, Vincent's whimpers gathered steam and he was seconds away from becoming inconsolable so I motioned him to follow me out to the hallway—away from the prying eyes of the class. "Get out your books and read."

"Now Vincent. I'm sorry you thought Santa Claus was coming today. I really am. But he's not. I think you misheard your dad. I'm sure he didn't mean for you to think Santa was coming today. It was just an honest mistake." I felt horrible for him. It *was* an honest mistake. His dad was working two jobs trying to keep their apartment while caring for Vincent and his two brothers by himself. He loved his two sons terribly and was doing a damn good job but they were one missed paycheck from being evicted.

"But I want him to come and fix my game!"

"I know, buddy. But you have to move on. Think about it—it's Valentine's Day! You're gonna get a bunch of candy and a bunch of cards. And between you and me—we're not doing anything new or that hard today. You guys are too excited. It's gonna be an easy day. Try and forget about the whole Santa thing. Just be happy that today is gonna be an easy school day. I mean we still have to do *some* work—but it won't be hard and they'll be coloring involved so you know it can't be *that* hard, ya know? Plus, with all your crying, you're all snotty in the nose and you know what that means, right?"

He slowly smiled.

Now I had to test him to make sure he was truly all right. "You want a Kleenex?"

He sniffed in hard twice. "No."

He was back on track—thinking like Vincent again. "That-a boy. Now get back to your seat and think about how your Valentine's envelope is not going to be able to hold all your candy. Did you see the back table? It's loaded! I've never seen so many treats! If fact, I'm glad Santa's not coming—that bulbous fellow would try to eat them all! Now go back to your seat and read so we can go to the bathroom, get through Social Studies and go to recess!"

With sixty minutes until the party, we were faking our way through our Social Studies lesson and, as usual, we were off topic within three minutes. Most of the time it was my fault but this time I only took half the blame. I was introducing the words *past*, *present*, and *future*. It was part of a lesson on what the word *History* meant.

"Who knows what 'past' means? Yes, Terry?"

"Means somebody dead. My Granny passed last year and my mama says my daddy says that why he goes out every night but mama says he just lyin'."

"Not quite."

"Uh uh. He go out every night. Mama has to sometimes get him off the porch 'cause he falls asleep out in the chair for he makes it inside."

"No…I mean, that's not what I mean by 'past'. But that is a way of saying that somebody has died—that they have 'passed' away, but it is spelled differently. And as far as your dad goes, it's been a rough year for him. He'll be all right. Yes, Almony?" You could always call on Almony. She was like a wild card in Uno. You could break it out when you were in tough straits.

"Past means it already happened. Like not right now."

"Yes! Perfect! Past means everything that has already happened. Last week is now *in the past*. Last year is *in the past*. Yesterday is *in the past*. This morning even—is already *in the past*. Even as I say this sentence—by the time you hear it and understand it—it's already *in the past*."

"Is that why…"

"Hand."

He shot up his hand quickly, bypassing the obligatory rolling of the eyes—he must have a really pertinent question. That was rare.

"Yes, Willy?"

"Is that why when I keep bugging my mom for this new video game that I've been wanting forever, she just keeps telling me I don't even play with the ones I got for the *past* Christmas?"

"Yes! The 'past' Christmas was the one a month or so ago, the one that *already happened*. Good, Willy."

"Now how about 'present'. What do you think that is? Yes, Vincent?" I was so excited to see his hand up to answer a question—I called on him immediately—not thinking what I had just said.

"It's something Santa brings you but it's only two of them and one is broken on the same day and then he never brings me anymore and he doesn't gotta work on Santa Valentine's Day to come fix it even though his name is in the day and he wears red."

Still an open wound. "Again, the word 'present' has a couple of meanings. It *can* mean a gift, like we would get on Christmas. It also means the time 'right now'—today or *this second right now*! And Vincent, again, I'm really sorry about the whole thinking-Santa-was-coming-today thing."

All I received in response was a turn-downed head, his stony silence, and quivering lips.

"Remember this, people: you can't do anything about the past. It's done. You can't go back. You can learn from it, but you can't change it. Forget about it." I was looking at Vincent now and he met my gaze.

"And the last word is future. The future is the time yet to come. It is an hour from now—when we're handing out our cards and passing out treats. It is a year from now—in this very room—having another *Saint* Valentine's Day party—but you will all be a little taller, a little older. The future is ten years from now—when you will all be young men and women in high school. We can't do anything about the future, either— just like the past. At most, we can plan for the future. But even then, you're only preparing what you think the future will be or look like. But no one can really predict the future. That can't happen.

"In between the past and the future is all that matters. That is the *present*. And that is the only thing you can control. Right here—right now. This very day—this very minute. You're here. No one is bossing you around—like your older brothers or sisters. No one is telling you to eat your vegetables—like you-know-who. You're warm—comfortable, we just had lunch a little while ago and I *know* you're not hungry or thirsty. No one is in any danger of getting hurt, and besides a little pressure on your tiny bladders, but what could be better than this? You could have it a whole lot worse than *right here—right now.*

"What you need to do is realize life is just a bunch of 'presents'. Not the gift kind—but the 'time' kind. Wherever you are—*be* there. You just have to remember—when you're in something that makes you feel great—be aware of it. Be *in it.*

"And the same goes for some time when you hate the 'present'"—like at the Dentist—or when you're getting a shot—or when your mom is making you stay at the table until all of your peas are gone. That's when the future comes in handy. You can always know that it will end. Because you know there will be a future. There *always is*. Just eat the peas quick and get out of that 'present'—that moment. Get to a new one—it might be better. Or you might just catch a double whammy and be ordered to the bath—*and although I don't understand why you wouldn't want to be clean*—I know you guys hate them. So just think of the time when you're *done*—all warm and snug in your bed."

That was a long one. But that is what caffeine will do to you sometimes—verbal diarrhea. When that happens, I am usually just happy if I didn't swear by accident. I usually take a quick ten seconds or so while they're staring—wondering if I'm done or just reloading—to quickly go over anything I said that might get me in trouble. Disclaimers were important.

"But—who knows? Do what you want. Whatever works for you. Yes, Marcus?"

"I went to the Dentist last week and I got three cavities. But they don't hurt so I don't want to go back for him to feel them."

"What are you talking about? Never mind. You have to go back. Or they'll just get worse. And he's going to *fill* your cavities—not *feel* them."

"Well, he said he was going to feel them. So…"

"Okay—whatever—you need to go back so he can *feel* your cavities."

We all broke down laughing at this—some of us not really knowing what we were laughing at—but we laughed anyway—it felt good and we meant it.

"All right—all right, quiet down. That was good." I stole a look at Marcus again. "*Feel* your cavities? What are you talking about? It's *fill* your cavities. Weirdo." He joined the kids' singing laughter as the tide picked up again.

"All right—that's enough. Now Marcus just gave us a *present*—a moment. Now it's gone—it's in the *past*. What's special about the past is that we can remember it—if we want to. It feels good. But it *is* in the past. We can remember it—but we can't be *in it* actually again. But that laughing 'present' is gone now. Maybe you'll get another. Who knows? Coats on! Line up!" They exploded in excitement—recess in February was unheard of. But the day was mild and a little running around before we gorged ourselves with candy wouldn't hurt anyone. Maybe the bus drivers, but they were a cranky lot anyway.

"But Mr. Thomas—we never go out in the winter. And what about our party?" Almony asked as she zipped up her coat, turned off the lights and grabbed the Recess pass to drop off in the office.

"It's not so cold today and we'll be back inside in a few minutes. I just want to get outside for a few minutes. Get some fresh air. We have plenty of time."

"Yay."

"Almony—wait." Motioning her towards my desk away from the prying ears of the others—half of which were busy being stymied by their zippers while the other half simply gave up with those dastardly metal teeth. "When we get outside—get everybody going in a game of tag or something. I gotta make a phone call."

"Did you forget to order the pizza again?"

"Shit! Yes I did! I'll call them first. Sorry for swearing."

"It's okay. I watch tv."

I did feel bad. As a class, we decided that the word "snickerdoodle" sounded like a swear word—so we sort of adopted it as our class swear word. It wasn't my finest idea as a teacher—but it wasn't the worst.

"Just keep Willy and them away from me for a few minutes. Which means you're gonna have to make him 'it' or he may not play and want to show me his new dance."

"He has a new one every day! And they're all the same!"

"I know—he's nuts. Just keep him away."

The wind wasn't stirring in the slightest and the sun was out, an incredibly fortunate February day. The kids were playing as if they hadn't been outside in three months—which they hadn't—and I was watching them in peace on the bench under a maple tree.

And then Willy saw me, must have thought I was lonely and decided to come over and keep me company.

"Almony! Almony!" I yelled, hoping she would corral him.

"Mr. Thomas. You wanna see my new dance I made up last night when my mom thought I was sleeping?"

"Lord no William! You have a new dance every day! I think Almony's calling you! I think she wants you to be 'it'. You better go check!"

He stood there in his dancing position, waiting for me to tell him to begin.

"Fine. Commence."

He remained in position one—waiting. "I don't have anything to say."

"What?"

"I don't have any comments to say. I just start dancing."

"Begin William."

It was all the same dance with minor adjustments each day. One day would be more arms than legs. Other times it would be all lower body and head. And on special occasions— like Mondays—when we didn't see each other over the weekend, he would break out the Jagger lips and strut with a strange sort of sideways shuffle. But today was a very special day. Apparently it was shake your ass day.

He did his usual routine but spent a considerable amount of effort in trying to make his backside bounce, craning his neck over his shoulder trying to watch it the whole time.

"You see my butt bounce?"

"Willy—you're gonna need to stop that right now. You're gonna hurt your neck. And I'm not explaining to your mom how you did it!"

"It's my butt dance. My mom says I dance good. She says I move well for someone my size. But I guess tall people can dance too!"

"Tall? Oh…yeah. Yes they can." Over Willy's undulating meaty shoulders I saw Antonio walking away from a despondent Vincent. Even Antonio couldn't shake him out of his disappointment. "Willy—go tell Vincent to come over here."

In a minute he was dejectedly sitting beside me.

"You gotta let it go, buddy. Think about what's happening here! It's Valentine's Day and we're outside for recess! That's unheard of! Plus—when we go in we're gonna eat pizza and not do any work! It's a great day!"

Sniffing in hard, he softly spoke, "It's a lot of good 'presents' at one time right now, right?"

"Yes, Vincent. And we'll see how long we can make this 'good present' last."

"Can I go to recess now?"

"That's what I've been waiting for."

"Are we gonna be at recess for a long more time?"

"It's all recess kid. It's all recess."

OVERCOMING DEBBIE GILROY
by Wayne Scheer

All his adolescent insecurities flashed before him as Arthur Mueller took Nancy Gomez's phone number from his wallet and placed it in front of the telephone.

I'm fifty-five years old, Arthur thought. I should be able to do this.

For the past thirty years, Arthur didn't have to. He was married, albeit not always happily. And marriage means you never have to ask anyone out on a date. You, especially, never have to make that dreaded phone call.

But he was divorced now. In the past year, he'd been on two dates arranged by friends. Neither worked out. Arthur thought of trying internet chat rooms, but he'd heard too many horror stories. Besides, it's bad enough being judged on your looks or your clothes or your job. Adding spelling and punctuation to the mix was too much.

He couldn't imagine hanging out at bars or going to a

senior's dance at the local Y. For a while, he thought of joining a church but decided that using religion as a pretext for finding a date for New Year's Eve had to be a sin more egregious than coveting your neighbor's wife or worshipping graven images. And they made the top ten.

So Arthur remained paralyzed, staring at the phone, half hoping Nancy Gomez would receive his telepathic signals and call him. He laughed, as he wiggled his fingers in the air and chanted aloud, "Call Arthur Mueller, Nancy. Call Arthur Mueller."

It didn't work. The phone remained silent and he began pacing like an expectant father. Or worse, like a teenager in heat.

Arthur knew how absurd he was. He looked over at his trusty mutt, Apathy, who, true to his name, was fast asleep on the floor, oblivious to his master's dilemma. As Arthur paced in front of him, Apathy opened one eye and allowed his tail a half-hearted wag. "Don't exert yourself on my account, boy," Arthur said. "I don't need your pity." The dog yawned, stretched and returned to his doggy dreams.

Images of Debbie Gilroy in her high school cheerleading outfit appeared as if she were a trapeze artist suspended in mid-air. He expected her to swing back to her perch. Instead, she just hung there in his mind, all smiles and glitter, waiting for him to catch her. But fifteen year-old Arthur Mueller dropped her with a clumsy telephone call.

"Hello, Debbie? This is Artie Mueller. You know, from English class. I sit in the back of the room. You sit to my right. No left. You're closer to the window and I'm sort of next to you in the next row. Yeah, that's right. The skinny guy with glasses. Uh, yeah, the one who laughs through his nose. I was just wondering if, you know, if, maybe, we could, umm, if you're not busy this Friday night, maybe we could…what? You have plans? Okay. Bye."

Arthur remembered how he avoided looking directly at Debbie after that, especially when he caught her and her friends pointing towards him and giggling together in the lunchroom.

But Arthur reminded himself that he was now a successful business analyst with two grown children. He was a middle-aged divorcee, for crying out loud, who wore contacts instead of glasses and hadn't laughed through his nose in years.

But no man ever outgrows his gawky teenaged self. "The world is divided into two types of males," he announced to Apathy. "The ones who played football in high school and the rest of us."

Apathy looked up at his master with eyes that bared his canine soul, expressing his deepest concern for the man who was, after all, his best friend. Walking towards the front door, he turned to glance at Arthur making sure he understood. "You woke me, dammit. Now walk me."

"Ah, procrastination. Good boy."

After a brisk walk, Arthur and Apathy returned to their battle stations. Apathy stretched out on the floor in view of Arthur and Arthur stretched out on a chair in view of the telephone. He checked his answering machine. "Nancy didn't call, boy. I guess it's my move."

He thought of Nancy's ready smile and soft, gentle voice. She was a little overweight and her hair wasn't always neatly brushed, but to Arthur that made her more real. She was funny and smart and worked in the cubicle next to his. Best of all, she was single.

His plan had been to ask her out at work, perhaps one evening when they both happened to be working late. But there always seemed to be somebody around. Before leaving work, he copied her home phone number from the company directory.

Arthur picked up the card on which he wrote her number and said aloud, "I'm too old for this." Apathy barked once in response.

Punching the numbers into his cell phone, he felt himself relax. When Nancy answered on the second ring he simply introduced himself, resisting the temptation to explain whether his cubicle was to the right or left of hers.

"Hi, Nancy. This is Art Mueller."

And after some friendly small talk about work and the weather, he put aside thoughts of Debbie Gilroy and asked simply, "Say, I was wondering if you'd like to get some drinks and dinner after work Friday?"

Without hesitation, Nancy said, "Sure. I'd like that."

Arthur imagined his hands closing confidently on Nancy's wrist as he caught her gracefully in mid air, both all smiles and glitter.

CAREER GIRL
by Carla Sarett

The other day, a young colleague from down the hall stopped by my office. She did not have work on her mind.

"Do you think it's wrong to develop relationships at work, I mean, do you think it's like self-destructive? Am I subverting my career?" She apparently was under the impression that her office romance was a high-security secret.

I played along. "Hmm," I said.

"I mean, this relationship could get serious," she said, darkly.

"I have a hunch it will," I let her know. "Call me psychic."

Later, I couldn't help but recall my first job in New York—right after college, in the grim recession of the '70s. I had been hired to write blurbs for children's books with names like Aunt Zelda's Flying Umbrella and The Tortoise Who Went to School. Actually, I merely re-wrote other blurbs from Publishers Weekly or Library Journal—and since I was never required to read the books, their insides remained a mystery to me. It was ironic, in a way, since I often praised them as "filled with the mysteries of childhood."

To make matters worse, I was a so-so typist. If all went well, Aunt Zelda's Flying Umbrella might remain "wistful" and "sweet." But, before computers, just one wrong keystroke ruined a whole page and, inevitably, wistful morphed into simple, and sweet to witty. My remedy was deep breathing. Breathe in, breathe out, I told myself, hoping against hope to achieve the sense of inner peace which everyone spoke about—but always eluded me.

Against all odds, my boss, Rita Greene, tolerated my lack of ambition and even made a stab at trying to be a mentor—within realistic limits, of course.

"Maybe next spring, you could come to the trade shows with me and meet the authors," she said, trying to perk me up. She moved her head from side to side, like a kindly doctor checking for signs of life.

I interpreted her comment as a scholarly one, intended for an audience with an interest in trade shows. I shifted gears. "Those are really great earrings."

She looked at me as if I had said something odd—and flew away to one of her many meetings, all speed and efficiency.

With Rita out of the way, I could turn my mind to daydreaming about dark-eyed Jeremy Levy who, inconveniently, worked two floors above me. It took creativity on my part to invent excuses to get upstairs, but I was up to that task, if no other.

One day, observing the stacks of manuscripts on Jeremy's desk and on the floor as well, I asked, "Are any of these interesting?"

And he said, "No."

I tried again. "But it must be fun reading them." I had no idea that they were mostly diet books and self-help guides.

He did not take the bait. "Not to me."

I noticed a tennis racket in the corner, which sank my spirits. Maybe Jeremy needed a doubles partner for a girlfriend—I was hopelessly un-athletic.

So, my progress with Jeremy had stalled, at least in the short term. But New York was a big city and that month, I met Peter Greene. Peter was attractive in a New York intellectual way—speaking in flowing sentences, like one of those surprisingly intelligent men in French movies. His passions were Marxism, politics and high quality audio equipment, perhaps in the reverse order, though.

We met at a lecture at The New School on the origins of anti-Semitism. Afterwards, we found ourselves on the same uptown bus and had drinks at a neighborhood bar with sawdust on the floor. In one of those New York-style moments, he recognized my name—it turned out he was Rita Greene's younger brother.

By another coincidence, Peter's apartment was only

three blocks from mine. He lived on East 80th in one of those sunless East Side apartments with brick walls and hardwood floors. There was no way to make such dim places cozy, and Peter hadn't even tried—everything looked brand new and untouched. We sat and listened to Sinatra. There was some discussion about the difference between cold digital sound, and the other warm sound—was it vacuum?

Grateful that I did not have to endure an evening of Led Zeppelin, I said, "It does sound warm."

The next morning, Peter called to ask me to lunch, if I had time. Of course, I had time. Since Peter was a graduate student, so did he. We walked to a Greek coffee-shop around the corner from my office—in hindsight, an unromantic choice, but in those days, the area around the Empire State Building offered little in the way of cute cafes.

Peter's meal-ordering process was complex and time-consuming. He vacillated between sandwiches and salads. He asked the tired waiter detailed questions about his culinary options. Eventually, he settled, nervously, on a grilled Swiss and fries—or number fifteen, in coffee shop-lingo. I was relieved to have that part of our meal over.

I smiled at Peter. "It was nice of you to call. I'm glad you did."

I was happy in a way. It was a treat to have lunch with a real companion and not sit alone at the counter. And I felt

Peter Greene and I had much in common, in the books and ideas department. I envisioned us together—maybe, debating Marxist theory over a glass of chilled white wine or attending a museum lecture.

He leaned toward me and said, "Bella, you're not my type, but I'm really into you."

"Your type," I repeated, taking it in. "I'm not?"

"Not really, no," he said, wiping his wire-rimmed glasses.

Instinct told me when men, especially men like Peter, had a type the girls in question were tall and blonde and wore cashmere and pearls. I quickly reviewed all of the types I was not: not tall, not short, not blonde, not red-headed, not almond-eyed, not to mention perky or cute. To be sure, it was long list.

I contemplated my newly discovered identity as a medium height, medium weight brunette with no defining features. Surveying the coffee shop, I saw more than a few twenty-something New York brunettes who could have doubled for me in a pinch; although, now that I bothered to look, they were better-dressed and thinner than I was.

These unwelcome insights made me glum. "I guess you're not my type either," I confessed.

Peter said, "What do you mean, I'm not your type. What's your type?"

I considered his question as the waiter placed plates on

the table. My college boyfriends had nothing in common, apart from the rather obvious fact that they ended up as ex-boyfriends. But being an ex-boyfriend hardly made them a type—or at least, I hoped not, since one of them seemed downright psychotic.

I said, "Hmm, maybe the kind of man who doesn't have a type. I think that's my type."

"That's the problem with feminism. Here I am, trying to give you a compliment–and you're twisting my words and distorting them," Peter said, in true debate-team style.

"Well, you see, that's the problem. I mean, a compliment is like, you're wonderful," I pointed out. "A compliment is you look nice in that sweater. That's a compliment. Anyway, I'm not a feminist, whatever a feminist is."

I delicately plucked a single French fry from his plate, as if to prove the point.

He pounced on my logic. "What do you mean you're not a feminist? You're just being facile, that's what women do to evade the issue."

"I think feminists like to work and I kind of hate work," I said, getting off track. "I mean, some women want to work, but I kind of wish I could just hang out or go see lots of movies. Maybe I would like to work one day a week, you know, for fun, like in a museum or something, or maybe not, maybe just read a lot. You know what I mean?"

My rambling grated on Peter. "Well, that's not the point. The point is, you, you're taking it personally like I was insulting you. So, you're not Marilyn Monroe. I mean, I came downtown to tell you what a great night I had."

I returned to my Greek salad. "It was a nice night," I agreed, more cheerfully than before. No girl could be Marilyn Monroe, after all—and it tickled me that Peter had resurrected her in the era of free love.

"Not that I want to marry you or anything," he continued, drowning his remaining French fries in a pool of ketchup. "Don't get the wrong idea."

The coffee shop became noisy with so many waiters shouting, number fifteen, fourteen, whiskey dry, it was hard to make myself heard.

"You know, my guess is this coffee shop's filled with men who don't want to marry me. Come to think of it, all of Manhattan's filled with men who don't want to marry me," I boomed so loudly that an older woman eyed me with alarm. She probably thought I was a hardened floozy.

"So now what? You're annoyed because we spend one night together and I'm not proposing? I mean, I'm not crazy or something where I'm going to ask a girl to marry me. I mean you don't expect that, do you?"

"Calm down, I don't want to marry you," I said. I meant to emphasize the "marry" part like a feminist—which I was not, but who cared? But, I ended up broadcasting the "you" part like an outraged lover.

I was sorry for my sharp tone. I had no license to tell Peter Greene that sex without love is just sex, even if you play music in the background; even if you think it's great sex, it's still just sex and men and women either move closer or further apart; there's no standing still. Who was I to tell anyone anything?

Peter jumped in before I could apologize. "So you don't want to." He acted as if he had proposed on bended knees, and I had cruelly rejected him.

"No, I don't," I answered. "We're just having lunch. That's all that's happening here. We're not talking about marriage. Actually, we don't even have a relationship, not a real relationship. Nothing's happening, nothing."

And it was then that I noticed Jeremy. He was ordering himself a sandwich to go, and he heard me turning Peter down, or so he thought. And this time, Jeremy looked at me and smiled, the barest hint of a smile, but it was enough for me.

Peter said, "So you're into someone else?"

I shrugged. Then I said, "Maybe."

"Unbelievable," Peter said, 'you are un-be-lievable. Rita told me you were crazy. She said you were kind of not really sane, like maybe on drugs or something, always tripping into things and coming in late and making excuses. She said you had problems and you're always sad and you have these headaches, and maybe you had a fall, and that's why you have these headaches, and you're always talking about the Holocaust. She said you might be crazy."

That was news, although it shouldn't have been. I had hardly proved a model employee. Rita had hidden her disdain well, though. She had been polite. That much, I had to grant her.

I said, "I didn't know, about Rita, I mean." I knew the part about myself all too well. I knew that part better than anyone.

Peter said, "Yeah, she wants to fire you, but she can't think a good reason to. She's had a hard year and she really needs someone she can count on."

"A hard year," I repeated, mostly to myself. "She's had a hard year."

Peter did not walk me back, which was just as well. I felt trapped between an apology and a complaint, without much feeling behind either. Besides, who knew what he might repeat to Rita who had already cast me as a lunatic—and a lazy lunatic, too.

After lunch, I marched into Rita's office and said, "So you don't like me, and you think I'm crazy." I didn't repeat the lazy part, since that was true.

She finished licking an envelope. Her voice was even. "Actually, I do like you. I just told Peter that you're doing a lousy job, and you are. You're smart, and there's no reason you couldn't do a better job. But I get it, the work's boring, the pay's not good. But you know these writers depend on us."

I made a helpless gesture of apology. "I know. I'll try, really, I will."

Rita looked faintly amused. "Maybe you will and maybe you won't. Anyway, it seems you spend all your time chasing after Jeremy Levy. But I guess he doesn't mind."

"He doesn't?" I said, forgetting all about the job and Peter and even Rita.

"Not from what I can tell," she said, shaking her head and opening another file.

Minutes later, I stood in Jeremy's doorway. I asked, "Do you have a type?"

He weighed my question like a puzzle. He pretended to scribble a few notes and I moved behind him—so he could smell my perfume. Then he stopped scribbling and we faced one another.

"Women. Women are my type," he said.

"So, I could be your type," I said, "I mean, with such broad parameters."

"What do you think?" he said in a way that made me blush.

"You might have told me." I almost said his name, but it felt too soon.

Jeremy smiled just as he had earlier in the coffee shop.

"I was getting around to it."

I turned away so I could try to breathe in and out. But he stood up and spun me around. He said, "What are you doing?"

I said, "Breathing, I'm trying to breathe. It's been a hard year, a really hard year. Sometimes it helps, I don't know, to slow down. I don't know. I actually don't know."

Jeremy said, "I don't mind, Bella."

For some reason, I'd run out of words. I made my upside down smile.

He said, "It's OK. Go back to your office, and I'll call you. Don't worry. Everything's going to be fine."

I returned to my wooden desk and a few minutes later, the phone rang. I picked it up before the first ring ended.

I heard Jeremy's voice. "Just start breathing and I'll listen." He sounded matter of fact, as if his request were perfectly routine, nothing out of the ordinary.

So I took a breath, and then another. My mind emptied as I breathed—I guess that was the inner peace that everyone talked about. Maybe deep breathing only works when someone else is listening, or when you know someone is listening. And I had the curious sense that he had been there all along, concealed from me, as if we'd been playing a children's game of hide and seek.

After a while, I whispered, "I guess I should hang up now."

Jeremy said, "No, don't stop yet—just keep on going. We're just getting started."

IN HER SHOES
by Lizzy Huitson

Greg was proud to say that he understood girls. He didn't understand politics or science or car engines, but he understood girls better than any of his mates. Growing up, he'd always been short (even now, he was only 5'5") and because of his height and the smattering of freckles across his nose, the girls at school had thought him cute and non-threatening. They let him into their world, and he found it to be an intriguing place. It was pretty, sweet-smelling and vicious, full of poisonous gossip and carefully-measured aggression. He explored this world thoroughly, using his newfound knowledge to get inside the minds (and sometimes the bedrooms) of girls he liked.

He often found himself acting as an agony uncle, dishing out advice wherever it was needed. This was particularly true with his roommate, Tony. Poor old Tony was eternally clueless about girls, and dragged a string of disastrous and short-lived relationships around with him like the chains of Marley's ghost.

Greg wasn't surprised when Tony stumbled into the living room one Sunday morning with a face like sour milk.

"Did Lucy stay over last night?" Greg asked, through a mouthful of toast.

"No," Tony mumbled, sitting down heavily in front of the telly.

Greg already knew that Lucy hadn't stayed over, of course. If she had, Tony would be looking even more disheveled than usual, and grinning like a nutcase.

"She said something weird last night," Tony continued, through a mouthful of Frosties. "She said I should get in touch with my feminine side. What's that about? Crying at all them rubbish chick flicks?"

Greg rolled his eyes. "No, just cuddle her when she cries at rubbish chick flicks."

"Really? Is that it? How's that getting in touch with your feminine side?"

Greg shrugged and chewed his toast thoughtfully, wondering how best to explain.

"The thing is, girls just want you not to take the mick out of their girly stuff. They don't want you acting like a girl. They want a real man, you know. Someone to protect them from...I dunno, burglars and spiders and stuff."

It had been a spider that had kick-started Greg's

relationship with Jess. They'd been on a very casual not-quite-a-date at the Up In Arms, when a hairy brown spider, about the size of a fifty-pence piece, had floated down from above like an ugly snowflake and hovered over Jess's head. When she caught sight of it, she froze, her eyes wide and jaw clenched in horror. Greg caught the spider in one deft movement with the aid of an empty pint glass and a beer mat. Jess had been reluctantly impressed. Six months later, she moved in with him and Tony.

Their one-year anniversary was coming up, and Greg was struggling to think of something to get her. She was difficult to shop for, since she wasn't interested in perfume or luxury bath products, and never wanted fancy chocolates because she much preferred Mars Bars and Kit Kats. Greg was so short on decent ideas that he had even asked Tony for suggestions. Tony suggested that since Jess was a fan of Kit Kats, Greg should buy four Kit Kat Chunkies, unwrap them, then wrap them all up together in silver foil to make a giant Kit Kat. Greg had liked the sound of that, but it didn't really seem like an appropriate anniversary present.

Eventually, he gave up and just asked Jess what she wanted. They were curled up on the sofa in front of the telly on a Thursday evening, and Jess was dozing on Greg's chest, warm and soft and smelling of peppermint shampoo.

"Mmm, not sure what I want," she murmured sleepily. "Something practical, maybe."

"You say that now, but when you open up your present and it's a year's supply of post-its and Tippex, you'll be disappointed," Greg warned.

"Well, something practical and pretty then."

"Oh, like heart-shaped post-its?"

Jess smiled and hauled herself into an upright position before settling back into the settee. She stretched her long legs out and discarded her heels. Greg didn't know why she bothered wearing them. They looked uncomfortable, and it wasn't as if she needed the extra height–she was a good two inches taller than him in her bare feet.

"Right, I'm admitting defeat," she muttered. "I know it's only ten but I'm knackered. I'm off to bed."

"OK, I'll be up in a bit."

Greg flicked through the TV channels, but there was nothing on. He found his eyes sliding back to Jess's high heels. They were really nice shoes, Greg mused. Jess looked sexy in them, and they were a good color, too. A glossy, cherry-red. As soon as he had the money for a first-hand car, he'd get one in that exact color. He looked at the shoes, then at the telly, then at the shoes again, then back at the telly, then put the shoes on.

He stared at his feet, as if he couldn't quite understand how they could possibly be crammed into a pair of three-inch heels that were only slightly too tight for him. They looked ridiculous with his thick grey socks, but he doubted they'd look any better without them—he had remarkably hairy toes.

Hesitantly, he pushed himself up from the settee, and was instantly delighted. He felt a little unsteady, but those three extra inches of height were fantastic. He finally understood what Jess was on about when she said a good pair of shoes made her feel confident. The good feeling disappeared very rapidly when Tony came into the room.

Greg expected Tony to laugh hysterically and rush to take blackmail pictures on his camera-phone. Instead, Tony looked him up and down slowly, raised an eyebrow and said,

"Mate, why are you wearing Jess's high heels?"

"I dunno. They make me feel tall. And...fierce."

"Fierce," Tony repeated, with an easily-discernible note of cynicism in his voice. "Fierce, like an animal?"

"Yeah, like a tiger. Or Beyonce. If Beyonce married a tiger and had a baby...It's that kind of fierce, ya know?"

"No, but never mind. Can you walk in those things?"

Greg doubted it, but he'd never been one to back away from a challenge. He took a step and wobbled dangerously, catching his balance just in time. Tony laughed, then offered Greg his arm, putting on his Victorian gentleman's voice and saying, "Allow me to assist, milady." Greg grabbed hold of Tony's shoulder and walked a few tentative steps, then a few more, and then a few more after that. Just as he thought he had the hang of it, his ankle twisted and he dropped like a stone.

"Don't tell Jess about this, yeah?" he said, rubbing his sore ankle.

"Don't tell her that you tried wearing her shoes, or that you tried walking in them and failed miserably?"

"Both. I didn't fail miserably though, I was doing fine until I fell."

"You know, most people consider staying upright to be a pretty crucial part of walking."

Greg scowled at Tony and said some very rude words.

Several times during the next few weeks, Greg found himself wearing Jess's cherry-red high heels. He never went looking for them if they were hidden away in the wardrobe–he told himself that would be weird. If they were lying around on the floor, though, or if they spilled out of the wardrobe on a wave of precariously piled junk when he opened it, he allowed himself to put them on.

Walking in them was like walking in stilts, so Greg told himself that he was learning a circus skill, not cross-dressing or developing a shoe fetish. Before long, he'd learnt to walk easily in them. Then he managed to walk in them while balancing a book on his head, and to kick a football around the kitchen while wearing them, and (after a couple of beers) to dance to Monster Mash while wearing them. He didn't tell Jess about his accomplishments. He suspected that she might be less than impressed.

He never wore the high-heels for long, but he started

getting sore patches on his feet nevertheless. He noticed that the shoes were also a little worse for wear. He'd stretched them out slightly–not enough for Jess to notice, but enough to make him feel a bit guilty. It was suddenly very obvious what he should get her for their anniversary.

Shoes were the ideal present. They were sort-of practical, but not too practical. He now understood the benefits of high heels, which included extra height and the comforting knowledge that one's shoe could be used as an effective weapon if necessary. Because of this, he felt ready to learn why girls enjoyed shoe shopping so much.

Unfortunately, he learned no such thing. The shoe shops were daunting, and he felt out of place and overwhelmed by the variety of colors and styles. Eventually, he ended up sitting cross-legged on the floor of the shoe section in Debenhams, eyeballing three different pairs of heels that were all vying for his attention. One pair was silver, with a strap that buckled at the ankle. One pair was shiny black, with dauntingly high heels. One pair was purple, with a little satin bow on the toe. They all *looked* right, but Greg knew, with frustrating certainty, that only one of them *was* right. There was only one way to find out.

With a quick glance around to make sure no-one was looking, Greg got to his feet and tried on each pair of shoes in turn. He walked a couple of steps in each pair, and became absolutely convinced that the purple ones were the best. He bought them without hesitation, too pleased with himself to notice the woman at the till giving him a funny look.

On the day of Greg and Jess's anniversary, Greg could hardly wait to give Jess her present, but Jess insisted on giving him his first. It was that aftershave that smelled like delicious things being cooked on a campfire in the middle of a pine forest. Greg thanked her, then urged her to open her own present. Her reaction was not exactly what Greg had expected.

As soon as she saw the shoes, she howled with laughter. Greg frowned in confusion.

"Don't you like them?"

"They're gorgeous," Jess assured him, once she'd finished laughing. "It's just so funny. I got you something else, you see...and it's...so similar."

She collapsed into giggles, then rummaged around under the bed. She emerged with what looked suspiciously like a shoe box. Perhaps she'd bought him some new running shoes.

"They're only Primark, I'm afraid," she said, handing him the box.

Opening it, he saw a pair of purple high heels. He made a mental note to use one of them to stab Tony to death the next time he saw him.

"They're the right size and everything," Jess promised. "Tony said you liked to wear my red ones when I'm not around."

"I just like the extra height," Greg mumbled.

"I love that you're short," said Jess. "And I love that you have such good taste in shoes. You don't need to bother hiding stuff from me, even the really bonkers stuff. I love you to pieces, always will."

"Oh. Well...that's good. I love that you're tall enough to get stuff off the top shelves when we buy groceries. And I love that you don't freak out about anything, except for spiders. And I'll always love you, too."

As Jess leaned in to kiss him, Greg suddenly felt ten feet tall.

CABRA
by D.T. Kastn

Rufus said, "There's a goat in the hall."

He said it again, too, because no one seemed to be paying him much attention. Or the goat, for that matter. It was a perfectly normal goat, of average size—for a goat—with a reasonably healthy gray coat the consistency of a shag rug. Maybe a little obtuse-looking but, again, this was par for the course when it came to goats. The other students appeared to be sidling past it, budging against the walls, as though it carried a dangerous curse other than the strong smell, which was—again—an integral part of its very goatiness.

Rufus approached the animal with caution. Everyone else was doing so—maybe there was something to it. Maybe it was a feral goat. A vampire goat. Maybe it was trying to get people to sign a political petition. Maybe it was a land-dwelling advocate trying to find help for its cousins, the goats of the sea—manatees. Or that was cows. Either way, this was a tricky proposition. Rufus sidled sideways up to it, ready to turn and run at the first sign of a charge.

The creature appeared pacific, however; the look in its mild golden eyes was bland and unassuming, generally sort of okay with everything, as though it had been drugged. Rufus assessed the situation.

"There's a stoned goat in the hall," he said. "Why is there a stoned goat in the hall?"

The expected response on any given day was, *Dude, it's college. Why should there* not *be a stoned goat in the hall? Or a gargoyle on the toilet, or twelve Mr. Rogers impersonators locked in the basement with a typewriter, or an experimental machine for controlling weather in the common room, making the coffee pot go on the fritz.* College had changed drastically since Rufus' first time around. It was the legalization of medical marijuana, he figured. Suddenly, everybody had back aches, but they were *very. Mellow.*

Much like the goat, in fact. Which nobody had offered an explanation for, not even the expected one. Maybe there was something else going on here. Everyone looked terrified. Rufus narrowed his eyes at the goat, and the situation in general. Something else—yes. Something else was definitely going on.

"Has anyone seen Milford?"

Still no reply, but the student who was squeezing himself past the goat—which had taken a step or two towards the wall, as though it was trying to make things awkward— suddenly developed a hurry.

"Gibze! Where's Milford?"

Gibze mumbled something incoherent and a voice floated down cloudlike to Rufus, a pronouncement from a higher power, the ultimate being: Milford's girlfriend, Katy, who wore pink and was terrifying. And possibly a ninja. There was a rumor going around. Rufus wasn't sure whether to believe it or not but the fact remained that he had once seen Katy take down a traffic cop whom she believed to have been mean to a puppy. And get away with it.

Katy slipped aimlessly down the stairs into Rufus' line of sight and greeted him with an engagingly sloppy grin. Her mouth always looked as though no thought had been put into it, as though it were the happiest happenstance, a peach tree in the wilderness. It was at strict odds with the rest of her. Katy was a highly trained individual and her body reflected all the control that exercise, diet, panty hose and a professional bra-fitting could offer. She also had no business being on campus without Milford.

"Where's Milford?" said Rufus, as coldly as possible. "You have no business being here without Milford."

"We're not joined at the hip, you know, Mr. King."

"But in that general vicinity," said Rufus. But his *voce* wasn't quite *sotto* enough and Katy flashed him a glare. He gulped, rallied his forces and went on. "There's a new charter, missy. Milford probably told you. No visitors without express permission."

"Which I have."

"And without official accompaniment."

"Milford's in the shower. He'll accompany me when he's clothed. Otherwise, that's against the rules, too. You all are so up*tight*. Just because of those couple of incidents in the last month—"

"The nudist streak, you mean? Or—the streak of nudists? Either way, I guess."

"You're going to have to help me with the goat. He's stoned out of his gourd."

Rufus had been momentarily distracted by semantics and synonyms; returning to what was passing for a conversation, he found that Katy had the goat by the scruff of its neck, like a recalcitrant kitten, and was trying to haul it to the door. The goat seemed to be content with its current lot in life, however, and wasn't keen on leaving the relative comfort of the hall.

"So it *is* your goat," Rufus murmured, eyes narrowed. Katy sighed.

"The next thing you're going to say is, *I suspected as much.*"

"I suspe—hey, why did you bring a goat in here, anyway? You're not supposed to be here. Why compound the offense by trailing your entourage of farm animals like you're some hopped-up pop starlet with meat on her head?"

This was a daring comparison to make, of course, because there *had* been that one ill-advised karaoke video.

"You are not making yourself any more likeable, Mr. King," said the possible ninja, in a voice that dripped with sweet danger, like honey laced with arsenic. She stepped deliberately towards him and he was suddenly, acutely aware of the fact that her pink heels were sharp stilettos; which, driven into a man's foot, would undoubtedly cause months of pain and silly lopsided dancing. Although he could legitimately file for medical marijuana at that point. He shrank back for a split second before realizing that she was still tugging ineffectually on the goat, and rallied himself again. He was always rallying himself when Katy was around. He might as well get fitted for a cheerleading outfit.

"I wasn't really trying to, to be honest," Rufus said.

"Let's leave your impolitic rudeness in the dust for the moment, shall we? Are you going to help me with this goat or not?"

Rufus slid his hands slowly, deliberately, into his pockets hoping this would be answer enough. It wasn't. She was still staring at him, waiting.

"Why should I?" he said. "Why not get someone else to do it?"

"Because everyone else is pretending I'm not here. It's like I'm a leper."

"Or a ninja," said Rufus, helpfully.

"Or a ninja with leprosy."

"Which would not help the ninja's stealth tactics,

much. If you leave a nose or a finger behind, people usually know you were there."

"Why do they treat me this way?" wailed Katy in a sudden excess of emotion. The goat eyed her askance. She loosed her grip on its nape, and it took two very deliberate steps away from her before she hurriedly grabbed it again. "Just tell me, Mr. King. You're the know-it-all."

"I'm a student advisor, if that's what you mean."

"So advise me."

"You're not a student!"

"Make allowances, Mr. King. Be a mensch, step up to the plate, pay it forward, play nice with others, and for God's sake grow a pair." She glared at him. It was infuriating. He was actually infuriated. He hadn't been infuriated for years. He hadn't been told to grow a pair for years, either. But at least his doctor had finally said, *No, really, it's a recognized medical condition.*

"They're terrified of you," he said, letting the fury speak for him. "They're terrified of you, because you're older than they are, and your hair is perfect, and you're beautiful, and you wear pink, and your very femininity is threatening considering we're not exactly co-ed, and you have no tattoos, and you smile at them, and you exude something which, though indefinable, is the very essence of everything they've ever dreamed of and everything they wake up wanting in the morning, like a warm girl with a hot cup of coffee and the world waiting in the palm of her hand. Also, you might be a ninja."

His fury was eloquent.

"I'm not a ninja, Mr. King," said Katy. "If I was, I could have got this goat in and out before any of you ever realized it. And then there would just be this inexplicable pile of goat do's in Milford's bed. And in his closet, too, although he wouldn't find that till later. He never bothers to clean in there."

"What?"

Katy closed her eyes, briefly. "There were a lot of points covered in those last couple of sentences. What didn't you understand?"

"Let's assume I understood everything perfectly, but repeat what you said anyway. Why is—why were you—what—"

"Why is the goat here? To leave a reminder of its presence in Milford's bed. Why were I doing that? That's hardly grammatical, Mr. King. No wonder you had to come back to college."

"It was a personal choice," said Rufus, but it was automatic. "What—"

"—happened?" prompted Katy. "I brought the goat in to help me say goodbye to Milford. I'm breaking up with him. I have broken up with him, actually, but the goat was intended as a sort of farewell gift. Unfortunately, he got loose and discovered Mr. Gibze's medical marijuana."

"He has a terrible backache," murmured Rufus.

"So I gather. Any other points you're unclear on?"

"Breaking up—"

"With Milford. Yes."

"Good—t"

"—bye. Yes."

"No," said Rufus. He was smiling strangely, the sort of smile a suicidal deer might give if caught in the headlights—loving its fate, welcoming it, feeling sweet relief in the very rushing wind of death. If deer could smile, of course, which was patently ridiculous. He was in college. He knew these things. "No," he said again, to make it perfectly clear. "*Good.*"

He allowed Katy a moment to take that in. She took it.

"So are you going to help me with this goat, or not?"

There was a reason all the students at Eastbrick were terrified of Katy. Terrified, and yet strangely drawn to her, Rufus noted. It was the sloppy smile, the unguarded turn of her mouth. Maybe it was even the impatient tapping of her death heels. Or was it, perhaps, the professionally-fitted bra? No, it was definitely the smile.

He cleared his throat.

"It's fairly obvious to me," he said, "that two people are needed to convince a goat to go up the stairs. Even when it's stoned. There's a mathematical equation in there somewhere. I know this. I'm in college."

Yeah, definitely the smile.

"You're going to help me," said Katy, softly.

"Well, you need an official escort," Rufus pointed out reasonably. "It's in the rules." He advanced on the seriously mellow goat and seized it by the scruff of the neck, like a fractious frilled lizard. "Come on, *cabra*. I'm also in Spanish 2."

"*Bueno*," said Katy.

"Show-off," said Rufus, glaring. "This is a task. This is a task and a half. I'm going to be half-starved by the time this is over. You should buy me dinner."

She peeled his fingers from the goat, replacing them with hers. "Is that so, Mr. King?"

"I could go for some barbacoa."

"Is that so," said Katy again, and tugged. "Get to the rear, Mr. King, and shove."

Rufus got to the rear. He shoved.

"Put your back into it," said Katy.

Rufus put his back into it. What did he care? This was college. Things like this happened all the time. It was one of the facts of life. There were probably rules about it.

Katy's grin was shining at him from over her shoulder, and a handful of strands had fallen loose from her artful coif.

"We made the first step," she said.

"Yes," said Rufus. "Yes, we did."

"Shut up, Mr. King," said Katy, but she said it in a sort of pleasantly threatening way. Rufus grinned, and he continued putting his back into it, and he gave it his all. All he had to give. Up the stairs, and to the landing, and to the promised land.

MORNING AFTER MONOLOGUE
by *Gabrielle Hovendon*

– Oh God, did I wake you up?

I'm sorry, I'm so sorry! You're getting up now though, right? Unless you want to go back to sleep. You can go back to sleep if you'd like. I have to go to work in a bit, but it's okay, you can go back to sleep. I trust you. I trust you here in the apartment while I'm gone. After all, I'd have to trust you to bring you home in the first place. Not that there's any reason I shouldn't trust you, I didn't mean to imply that. Oh, okay, you're getting up.

– What would you like for breakfast? Can I fix you something?

If you tell me what your favorite breakfast food is, I'll try to make it. No guarantees, though, especially if it's something foreign. I tried to cook falafel last week and it burned the pan and I had to throw it out. You don't look like the kind of person who eats foreign food for breakfast, but I'm not certain. Are you a toast kind of guy? How about cereal? Are you one of those people who slurps up the milk after you've finished the cereal? I am, but it's okay if you're aren't. What about bacon? Do you like bacon? Okay, I guess I can surprise you.

– The shower's right through there. Towels are in the closet on the left.

Unless of course you don't want to shower. Oh God, you'll think I think you smell bad, and that's not what I think at all. Of course, I haven't smelled you since last night, but you smelled fine then. Good, not fine. Fine implies you didn't smell good, and you did. But if you want to shower, I promise I won't think it's because you smell bad. Some people just like to shower every morning, regardless of smell. It's not my cup of tea, but far be it from me to–tea! I forgot to ask if you wanted some tea or coffee with breakfast! Hold on, can you hear me with the water running in there? If I sort of yell through the door, can you maybe tell me if you prefer sugar or creamer? No? What if I open the door a crack…

– Oh God, you're not in the shower yet! I'm so sorry, I thought you'd be behind the curtain!

Did you see me looking? I know you heard me, but I think you saw me looking, too. Quick, should I pretend I didn't see you or just make a joke? Oh, God I saw your penis and everything. It wasn't on purpose, I swear! Only, did it look like that last night? Obviously the situation was different and it was dark and everything, but I don't remember it looking quite like that. I mean, I don't think it's ugly or anything, I just remembered it differently. Do you think I'm being creepy? I'm not trying to be creepy. I saw everything last night, it shouldn't be creepy if I accidentally walk in on you naked. This isn't like the locker room—no surprises here. What was the joke I was going to make? Oh, you're getting out of the shower now?

– This is really embarrassing, but I don't think I remember your name. Keith, right, right. Sorry!

I was going to look through your wallet but then I thought you might come back into the room and it would look weird, like I was trying to steal your identity or something. Of course maybe you'll think it's weird that I'm thinking this now. Or maybe you'll think it's weird that I think it's weird that I'm thinking it. Or maybe… ha-ha, it's like a whole chain of weirdness. You know what it's like? It's like one of those halls of mirrors where things keep reflecting back on each other, but with weirdness. Hall of weird mirrors. Mirrweirds. Weirrorness.

– I'm sorry, I think I got a bit of shell in the eggs when I was scrambling them.

I tried to pick it out but I couldn't find it again, so there's going to be some shell on one of our plates. One of us is going to bite down on that eggshell. I'm sorry, I should have just hardboiled them, but some people don't like hardboiled eggs and I figured… Well, which plate are you going to take? Okay, but the shell might be in that one. I'm not saying it is, but it might be. Just so you know. There's really no way of

telling, that's the thing. Unless I made a new batch, of course.
Do you want me to make a new batch? God, I should have
thought of that in the first place. That's what I'll do. I'll make
a new batch. After all, who wants to be the one who gets the
eggshell? If it's you, you'll think I didn't like you enough to
give you the good plate, but if it's me you'll think I took it for
myself on purpose just to be nice, and that's really not the kind
of girl I am. That's not the kind of girl I am at all.

    – Wait, you're leaving?

    Why are you leaving? Did you get the shell after all?
You don't have to keep eating it, I'll make something different!
Or did you want something else to drink? I knew it. I should
have offered you the orange juice. Or is this about what
happened in the bathroom? I meant to explain better, but I
promise I wasn't trying to look at you. Not that you're not
worth looking at, that's not what I mean. I wouldn't have
brought you here last night if you weren't worth looking at—
but not in a superficial way. I don't want you to think I only
care about appearances! It's just I don't usually peek at men
when they're in my shower. I don't ever peek at men in my
shower. I don't know why I said usually. Not that I've even
had that many men in my shower, because I haven't. But if I
had, I wouldn't have peeked at them.

    – Keith, please wait!

    Oh God, it must be because I forget your name. That's
it, isn't it? That has to be it. What kind of girl forgets the name

of the guy she brings home? It's like something the dumb lead in a romantic comedy would do, only it would all work out in the end for her. Not that I think this isn't going to work out, I just wish you'd stop putting on your shoes and everything. What was that one movie where the girl had amnesia and mixed up her boyfriend with this total stranger? Oh God, the b-word! I'm so sorry, I swear I wasn't thinking that way at all. It just slipped out, sort of like last night with your... Oh God, I shouldn't have brought that up that either! You're probably still embarrassed about it. Are you still embarrassed about it? Anyway, I don't even want a boyfriend, really. I mean I like you, I just don't want you to feel like there's any pressure. There's no pressure, okay? Although if you did want to be my boyfriend I promise I'd remember your name. Keith, see? I remember it already!

    – Wait, what?

    I don't understand—you're saying that I'm too quiet? That this morning was like waking up next to a monk? Are monks even quiet? I thought they went around singing chants and preaching to animals and stuff, or is that friars? Is there even a difference? And hold on, you're not saying I'm like a monk in bed, are you? God, what if I'm going bald on the top of my head and don't even realize it? And what if—Keith, come on! Please don't go! I can start talking more! Look, I'm talking more right now!

    – Won't you at least stay for some coffee?

And do you want sugar with it? I'll go get the sugar, and then maybe you can explain how I'm too quiet. Do you want creamer? I'll get the creamer out, too.

– Oh, you're late for work?

Who has to work on a Sunday morning?

– Of course. I'm fine, really I am.

It's just a surprise to hear you say I'm too quiet, that's all.

– Yeah. See you around, I guess.

Because sometimes I feel like I never shut up.

RALPH'S RUSE
by Jim Harrington

"Oh, my God. She's going to do it."

Ralph looked up from his jigsaw puzzle to see Millie peeking out the family room window. When the clap of thunder rattled the windows, he dropped the piece it'd taken him forever to find.

"Do what?" Ralph said. He located the elusive piece and locked it in place. After forty years of marriage, he knew how animated Millie could get over nothing.

Millie turned to him.

"Remember how Suzanne told us about Albert's wish to die on the golf course if he got too sick to take care of himself?"

"Yeah. So, what about it?"

"Well, he must be sicker than we thought. She's pushing him in a wheelchair onto the fifteenth fairway, and she's got something in her hand." Millie pointed at the window. "Get over here and see for yourself."

Ralph pushed himself to a standing position, knowing

Millie would keep after him until he obeyed. He walked on stiff legs, bent at the waist. He'd sat too long working on the puzzle.

"Maybe they're just being frisky," Ralph said, as he approached the window. A light along the street opposite the green expanse provided enough illumination to see the two figures.

"Really, Ralph. At their age?"

"Yes, at *our* age," Ralph mouthed behind Millie's back.

Invigorated by the brief walk and the sight of his neighbors, Ralph reached out and pinched Millie's bottom. She slapped his hand away and gave him a look. Ralph stepped to one side and peered through the spotless glass.

"Don't stand right in front of the window. They'll see you," Millie said, pulling him halfway behind the curtain. "Oh my. Is Albert naked?"

Ralph squinted at the couple. "He must have shorts on. Can't really tell, though. It's kinda dark."

"I think he's naked," she said. He turned to see Millie looking through the binoculars she used for birding. "Oh my God, he *is* naked."

Ralph didn't know how she could tell, but he knew better than to argue. "How about Suzanne. Is she naked, too?"

"Ralph. That's disgusting," Millie said and gave him that look again.

"Geez, did you see that lightning?" Ralph said to

change the subject. "She better turn him around and get inside."

As they watched, Suzanne bent down, first on the right side, and then the left.

"Looks like she's putting the brakes on," Ralph said.

Millie stood speechless, a hand over her mouth.

"And now she's putting something in his hand," Ralph said and moved closer to Millie. "It looks like a 6-iron. What the hell is she doing?"

"I don't know, but I think you should call the police."

"Wait. Let's see what happens." Ralph put his arm around Millie's waist.

"The storm is getting closer," Millie said, pointing to the western sky. She shifted her slender body into him. "We should do something."

"Wait," Ralph said. "I'm sure everything will be fine."

They watched Suzanne put the club in Albert's left hand and raise it as high as his arm would go. At that moment, a bolt of lightning struck a nearby tree. Suzanne fell to the ground and covered her head. Albert rose from his chair and yelled to the heavens, the club held high. Millie turned into Ralph's arms. This was better than he could have hoped for.

"OH MY GOD," Millie said. "He's...he's...huge."

"That is quite a boner." Albert lowered his hand to Millie's rear and gently rubbed up and down. He waited for Millie to say something. Instead, she swayed her body against his caress.

"Ralph."

"Yes, dear."

"I..." Millie put a hand on Ralph's chest and smiled. "Let's go upstairs."

Ralph put his arms around Millie, pulling her body to his, and gave a thumbs-up sign through the window. He didn't know if Suzanne and Albert could see him or not, but he'd be sure to tell them how well the skin-colored body suit and ten inch strap-on dildo had worked.

SPORKED
by Micaela Gardner

When Marvin decided to break up with his girlfriend of four months, Mary-Anne, he knew there was bound to be some hurt. What he didn't expect was Mary-Anne stabbing him in the belly with a plastic spork.

"Oh my God! You messed up my to-do list! I wasn't supposed to stab you until after lunch!" Mary-Anne wailed, her gray eyes filling with tears. "You derailed my whole day. I had two thirds of my tasks done already—sixty-six percent, to be precise."

Marvin considered calling the police or an ambulance or something, but Mary-Anne had her car, and she still had all of his CDs in it, so he reluctantly accepted a ride to the urgent care center that was located three blocks away. It was better than walking.

He probably could have gone without a trip to the doctor if Mary-Anne hadn't leaned forward and rotated the spork one-hundred and eighty degrees, pushing the spork so far into his belly that a passerby would not be able to identify what utensil had penetrated him in the first place.

"I didn't mean to do that," Mary-Anne said as she accelerated through the stop sign, nearly hitting a pregnant woman with a stroller. "I just—you said those things, and they made me so mad, those clichés—really, darling, it was the clichés that got hurt."

Marvin considered asking her if she thought the clichés were bleeding out through their belly buttons and hurt like holy hell too, but decided aggravating her further would not be a wise move.

"In a way," she said, "I think you should be flattered. I mean, who else would risk your life for you? Who else would love you so much, that if she couldn't have you, no one could?"

Marvin thought back to Becky, his last and only girlfriend before Mary-Anne. Sweet, dense, Becky with her frizzy brown hair who looked like a little brown bear that walked on its hind legs. For Marvin's nineteenth birthday, Becky bought them two puppies and named them Salt and Pepper. She thought it was a step forward in their relationship. Marvin had broken up with her almost immediately, the thought of taking care of animals with his girlfriend more frightening than being stabbed in the stomach with a spork. The cutesy, matching names disgusted him on a visceral level. The last Marvin had heard about Becky was that her apartment couldn't keep pets, and she had gotten rid of them and bleached her hair dandelion yellow and started sleeping with guys named "Mike" and "Adam". These escapades were all bitterly recounted on her Facebook, which he was ashamed to say was public to his parents.

"If you think about it, being stabbed is a very common literary theme. Juliet stabbed herself when she found Romeo dead. See, baby, we're like Romeo and Juliet." Mary-Anne gave Marvin one her of trademarked, quivering half-smiles, completely insane but also the single most arousing sight Marvin had ever witnessed.

The pain in his stomach seemed to lessen as they parked the car in the lot.

On the examination table, Marvin thought about how when he broke up with Becky, he got nothing. She didn't even cry in front of him. Granted, he later found out about her crying, mostly through Facebook status updates and her Twitter account ("Becky White is sobbing uncontrollably after losing the single most important person and two most important puppies all in one day"). But he didn't get the drama he had anticipated, which was both a let-down and a relief.

But Mary-Anne had given it to him.

"I think we should see other peo—"

The cliché had only partially started tumbling out of his mouth when Mary-Anne seized his gravy-covered utensil and thrust it into his quivering belly.

At first he felt nothing at all as he stared down at the white plastic handle sticking out of his abdomen. Then the pain set in, and the blood began to soak through his plain white t-shirt.

Mary-Anne, the single most selfish woman he had ever met in his entire life, suddenly sacrificed all of her white starchy napkins to the cause of his bleeding stomach.

And really, she didn't have to drive him. Wasn't there something tragically poetic about being hurt by the person you love most, and then being healed by them? Marvin stared at the watercolor painting of a daisy as his legs swung back and forth, hanging over the floor.

His father used to tell him that what scares you most is usually good for you. He had used this philosophy to teach his son to eat vegetables, how to ride a bike, and to study his geometry homework. But doesn't this apply to love, too? Isn't the idea of loving someone, of getting stabbed in the belly (metaphorically or otherwise) scary as hell but, in the end, worth it? No, he would not live in fear. Marvin loved vegetables and rode his bike every day to school, where he majored in math. A slight mishap like a spork in the belly would not intimidate him from pursuing true love!

The doctor bandaged up his stomach and prescribed him horse pills that were supposed to help with infection. Marvin was supposed to take three pills a day for eleven days, but he assumed he would forget to do so in less than a week.

Mary-Anne was in the waiting room, clutching a *Highlights For Kids* magazine and staring at him with wide eyes.

"Babe, I'm so sorry," she gushed. "Please, forgive me. I just don't know what got into me."

Marvin took the magazine out of her hands and carefully put it down on the table. Mary-Anne slowly rose out of her seat.

"I think we're at a point in a relationship where we can start thinking about adopting some puppies," he told his girlfriend, the love of his life, as he held both of her hands in his own.

At once, Mary-Anne flushed with surprise and delight.

"Oh, that would be lovely! What will we name them?"

"How about Bonnie and Clyde?" he asked her as they walked through the automatic sliding glass door.

"Oh God, Marvin, sometimes I love you so much it hurts," Mary-Anne exclaimed as they walked towards her beat-up, old Mercedes Benz.

"Me too," Marvin said, wincing with each step towards his girlfriend's car, "me too."

OF WOMEN'S WILES AND UNDERWEAR
by Michael A. Tashjian

First off, I want to inform you that I am *not* gay. I like girls—a lot—which is exactly what compelled me to pick up the magazine. I was at the doctor's. Lately, my mom had been puking and getting dizzy, so she set up an appointment and made me go with her. I thought that was stupid, since all I did was sit in the waiting room the whole time. I was looking through a pile of *Time, People, and Readers' Digest* when I spotted a picture of Jessica Alba peeking at me from underneath the out-dated issues. It was one of those teen girls' magazines. Printed on the cover were things like, "This Year's Trendiest Back-to-School Outfits," "New Workout for Your Abs," and one shout-out in bold letters: "How to Get His Attention." *That's interesting.* I scanned the room first—there were only old people around—so I picked up the magazine and flipped to the indicated page.

It wasn't at all what I expected. There were three paragraphs filled with little secret tricks for girls to use. The first one was entitled "At the Laundromat." Specific steps followed. "When unloading delicates from the dryers, lift lingerie and scrutinize at eye level, as if examining…" *How stupid. What kind of girl would use this?* The next paragraph was entitled "At School," and detailed techniques were listed on how to smile, giggle, "bat the eyes," and other weird stuff. The last trick was some kind of "hallway glance" and I was just getting into that when my mom reappeared and said it was time to go.

* * *

She announced at dinner that she was pregnant. My dad and I had suspected for a while, so we weren't too shocked. By five months, though, my mom was at the point where she had to waddle everywhere she went, so we decided to sell some of her clothes that didn't fit anymore. It was Garage Sale Day in the neighborhood, and I was helping her carry some stuff out to the drive way when in one box, I noticed some small, lacy underwear. "You have got to be kidding me," I said.

"What?"

"You're going to sell your *underwear* at a *garage sale?*"

"Well, why not? They're perfectly good panties." She obviously saw no problem with it.

"Mom! That's gross! Nobody around here is going to buy your old underwear!"

"We'll see about that," she retorted. "Five dollars?" She had a weird way of ending arguments. *Kind of immature*, I thought, *but whatever.* I took on the deal.

It'd been three hours since I'd set up the tables, and no one had come even close to buying the underwear. I was looking forward to the five bucks with confidence when a girl I'd never seen before showed up. She had straight brown hair that sort of covered her eyes and a slim figure. I took the opportunity to stare while Mom was inside. Taking no notice of me, she skimmed the tables, coming dangerously close to my mom's abominable lingerie. *No, no, no, no, no!* It quickly caught her attention, and she smirked as if amused. Good. She thought they were ridiculous too. Mom came outside then, and saw my jaw drop as the girl picked up the lacy thing and inspected it at eye level where it dangled from her manicured fingers. What shocked me even more than her interest was— could she possibly be using the "laundromat technique" on *me?* Did it count at a garage sale?

I tried not to look when the girl said, "How much for these?" Mom hobbled over to the table all too quickly, and said, "Twenty-five cents." The girl took out the money, paid, and left.

With a triumphant smile, my mom waited next to my lawn chair, hand outstretched. I sighed, and dug around in my pocket for a while until I came up with five dollars. She chuckled, taking the cash, then pointing out haughtily, "I've already earned back twice of what I paid for those," she shuffled away with her hand on her globular belly.

* * *

I couldn't believe my luck a week later when freshman year started. That girl had English class with me and, even better, we ended up being partners for some big project. Every day we sat across from each other and plenty of "eye-batting" and radiant smiles took place. I couldn't believe it. She liked me.

On Friday, when the bell rang to end sixth period, all of the classmates pushed through the door and swarmed into the hallway like bees. She passed me. She always does, but this time, she looked back, shot me a mysterious glance with a mischievous smirk, and turned around the corner. It was perfect. Did she practice in the mirror or something? It's so weird—the steps girls take to get a dude's attention—but they work. I'm fascinated.

But there's just one thing, whenever I'm with her...I can never help wondering if she's wearing my mom's underwear

SQUIRREL CHIPMUNK LOVE

Excerpted from: Unselfpublished, a memoir by Michael
Kimball

by Michael Kimball

Editor's Note: *I first encountered* Unselfpublished, a
Memoir by Michael Kimball, *by Michael Kimball, during my time in
the Stonecoast MFA program at a faculty reading. Before reading,
Michael gave a bit of context to help the audience understand the
transformation that had occurred in his writing.*

*Apparently, Michael wrote the piece in response to another
author by the name of Michael Kimball who was publishing overseas
under the same name. This faux Michael, as we shall call him, was a
terrible writer and, as if that wasn't bad enough, was publishing without
including an author photo. Readers apparently confused the two authors,
as there was no way to distinguish the best-selling Michael Kimball from
the impostor without a photo, and as a result the real Michael Kimball's
sales took a tumble.* Unselfpublished *was his response. It utilizes the
worst writing techniques and tropes to great comedic effect and is the best
bad writing I've ever encountered. Make no mistake, every cliché and
misplaced modifier is intentional, and Michael Kimball is a genius.*

I hope you enjoy the piece as much as I do.
Oh yeah, and pellets = pharmaceuticals.

Yes, it is I, squirrel. Earlier in park I shared the rest of my pellets with 1) female chipmunk, 2) male mouse, 3) cat, indeterminate sex, and they came back for more, which we also shared because I actually found some more pellets in my pouch (squirrels have pouches, some), and sat together on the bench to watch cars until the cat and mouse paired up and went away, leaving the chipmunk behind and me haunted by Johanna, and now when that Chipmunk looked at me with those chipmunk eyes all I could see was Johanna, and when she brushes her hot fur against mine, all I can feel is Johanna. Johanna. In the present tense. Johanna. So I brush her back. Not her actual back with an actual brush. I rub my furry leg against her furry leg, and a very unusual sensation overtakes my soul.

What care I what specie she is? Hot animal desire has invaded my brian and so roughly I take her in my arms and kiss her with my lips while her hot breath from her nostrils rang like jackhammers in the insides of my ears. When our moist tongues touched, fiery hot electricity jolted through my compact body straight to the throbbing manhood of my being which shot up like a real man's penis but not as large, especially when I felt her furry breast with my throbbing fingers and opposable thumbs. When I pull her tail, she remarks hotly, "Yes! Yes!," wiggling her brown and tan and other shades of body beneath me like a small excited woman. "Do it now, Nick! Oh God. Do it now!"

How she wanted me. And how I wanted her, but I could tell she was inexperienced and needed to be educated in the lusty lessons of love. "Do you trust me?" I queried.

"Oh YES!" she cried. "Do it, Nick! Do it NOW (even though it would be sodomy)!!"

"Oh, no," I disagreed. "Webster's Dictionary defines SODOMY as oral OR anal copulation with a member of the same or opposite sex; OR copulation with an animal."

"And I'm a chipmunk," she pointed out to me.

"And I'm a squirrel," I pointed out to her back. "Clearly, Webster was a human, and meant it would only be sodomy for him to copulate with a squirrel. OR chipmunk."

"Oh. Now I understand," she said, understanding. "But what about," she inquired, "oral?"

"Webster only said it was sodomy," I explained. "He didn't say it was wrong."

She looked at me with excited breasts. "Yes, Nick, yes! OH YES!" she gasped as she started doing something to my manhood which I've only seen dogs, collars merrily jingling, do to their own. "Oh Nick!" she chattered, "Nick! Nick! Nick! Nick! Nick! Nick Nick Nick Nick!!"

"No, please," I pleaded, "don't talk," and so she stopped talking and we writhed in sweet ecstasy and then pain when we rolled off the bench and hot gravity pulled us down to rock-hard concrete, which was the sidewalk, and she squeaked, "OOFF!" and started to run, but I caught her tail and pulled her back. (By the tail.)

"Oh, yes! Yes! Yes! Yes! Yes! Yes!" she agreed, as I pulled her underneath me and delved into the depths of her dark desire with machinegunlike motions of my manhood, and other rapid movements.

"Oh, Nick, do it!" she cried. "Do it! DO IT! DO IT!!"

"I am," I assured her.

"Do it better!" she cried and slapped my face.

"This much better?" I inquired, slapping her back – her actual back, as one might greet an old friend.

And then . . . suddenly. . . she emitted a large gasp. I felt her stiffen.

"AHH . . . AHH," she began, like a woman or animal on the edge a very high cliff that has lost its balance, with arms waving excitedly. "AHHH . . . AHHH," she exclaimed and then all at once she screamed in a very loud voice, "Ahhhhhhhhhhhhhhhhhhhhhhhhhhhhhhh-AH!"

For she was enjoying her climax! So I ran up a tree.

FALLING
by Stone Showers

Donny Carrino was thinking about sex when he fell from the thirty-seventh floor of the International Mega-Bank of Commerce Building. Specifically, he was thinking about how he had just had sex with Christy from accounting, and how his wife would likely be very angry with him if she were to find out about it. (Donny hated it when his wife found out about his occasional infidelities. She had exceedingly good aim when she was angry, and Donny bruised very easily). Of course, the way Donny saw it, his wife was truly the one to blame for what had just happened. After all, if she had attended to his needs that morning as he had asked, then Donny would have had no need to cheat on her with Christy from accounting.

Donny smiled to himself. He liked it when he could blame his wife for his indiscretions. It always made him feel somewhat better about himself. Unfortunately, this feeling of self-congratulation didn't last very long, for it was at that very instant that Donny stepped off the thirty-seventh floor of the International Mega-Bank of Commerce Building.

Now, Donny was not as terrified as you might imagine. Rather, he was angry at himself for having made such a silly mistake. He was also worried that he would eventually have to fill out a boatload of paperwork explaining this mistake to his superiors. You see, Donny was the junior assistant project manager for the construction firm that was building the International Mega-Bank of Commerce Building. As part of his duties, whenever someone was injured or killed on the job, Donny had to fill out dozens of forms explaining how the accident happened, who was to blame, and how such a thing could be prevented in the future. Donny hated filling out these forms. He hated it even more than explaining to his wife why he had been forced to cheat on her.

Now Donny was no physicist, but he understood how gravity worked. He even knew a thing or two about aerodynamics. (Donny liked to watch the Discovery channel after having sex.) It was for this reason that Donny spread his arms and legs out as wide as possible. By increasing his drag coefficient, a term he had learned from the Discovery Channel, Donny hoped to slow his descent and give himself more time to think. Doing a quick calculation in his head (Donny was very good with math) he estimated that he had just a little over four seconds before he reached terminal velocity. Coincidentally, this was also how much time he estimated remained before he reached the ground. Donny found the congruence of these two facts somewhat ironic.

Now, you may be wondering at this point if it is true that people's entire lives flash before their eyes in situations such as this. It isn't, at least not in the way that most people think. When faced with imminent death, most people tend to think only about the things that matter to them most.

Donny thought about sex.

Donny's wife said he was addicted to sex. After she caught him cheating for the third time, she even made him join a therapy group for people with similar predilections. She said she hoped he would learn something from it. And he did. Donny learned that sex addict therapy was a great place to meet women. In fact, by the end of the first month Donny had managed to have sex with seven of the eight women in the group. Of course, when Donny's wife found out about this she made him stop going to the sessions.

Women could be so fickle.

Donny used to buy his wife diamonds when she caught him cheating. But this became rather expensive, and also dangerous. Diamonds—especially the larger variety—hurt when his wife threw them at him. (Remember, Donny's wife had very good aim.)

More recently, Donny took his wife on extravagant trips when she caught him cheating. This had two advantages. The first was that it limited the number of projectiles available for his wife to throw. (The hotels that Donny preferred were those that bolted everything—lamps and remote controls included—to the tables.) The second advantage was that there tended to be a large number of attractive and available women in these hotels (Donny liked going to places where there were lots of attractive and available women).

The last time Donny's wife had caught him cheating he took her to New Orleans for Mardi Gras. This was a place, Donny knew, where some women drank more than they should, and then took their shirts off for no reason at all. (And yes, Donny liked it when women took their shirts off. It usually meant that they wanted to have sex with him).

Unfortunately, Donny's wife did not want to go to the place where these things were happening. Instead, she insisted that they go see a voodoo medicine woman that one of her friends had told her about. Seeing as how his wife had caught him cheating on her only three days before, Donny had little choice but to agree.

The medicine woman was younger that Donny would have expected. She wore an outlandishly colorful headdress and rings on every finger. When she spoke it was with a thick Creole accent.

"What is eet I can do for you?" she asked. Donny, of course, had several ideas about what she could do for *him*, but he was smart enough to keep these to himself. His wife, on the other hand, spoke right up.

"I'm looking for a way to keep my husband from cheating on me," she said.

The medicine woman eyed Donny with newfound suspicion. "You be a wanderer, ay?"

Donny shrugged. It would have been pointless for him to deny it at this point.

The medicine woman turned back to Donny's wife. "I 'av just da ting for you then," she said. The medicine woman held out a small amulet hung from a black cord. The figurine resembled a man when looked at from one side, but looked distinctly like male genitalia when turned around and viewed from the other.

Donny's wife giggled. "Is this one of those dolls you stick pins into?" she asked.

Donny cringed at the image this conjured.

"Nah. Dose is just garbage for da tourists. Dis is da real ting."

"Perfect," Donny's wife said. "Tell me how it works."

The medicine woman looked Donny up and down for a moment and then turned back to his wife.

"You wear dis around your neck, and when he cheats," she nodded toward Donny. "When he cheats, it will spin around tree times."

"You don't say?" Donny's wife smiled. "And what do I do then?"

The medicine woman jabbed her hand out toward

Donny, making scissor motions with two of her fingers. "You cut it loose," she said.

Donny's wife giggled once more. "I cut it loose? Do you mean the figurine or something of Donny's?"

"Eeder one will do. Da trick is to cut it loose as soon as possible." She looked at Donny and smiled. "You cut it loose and let it fall. Then—" the woman shrugged. "No more cheating."

This entire line of conversation made Donny very uncomfortable, and despite the fact that the medicine woman was clearly coming on to him, Donny ushered his wife out of this shop as soon as she had paid for the amulet. Indeed, Donny was so disturbed by this visit to the medicine woman that he did not cheat on his wife again for the remainder of their trip. In fact, he did not cheat on her again for an entire week after that.

Not until Christy from accounting that is.

As Donny plummeted past the seventeenth floor of the International Mega-Bank of Commerce Building he wondered if the amulet his wife had purchased might have something to do with his current predicament. Of course, Donny did not believe in such things as voodoo magic. He was, after all, the type of man who watched the Discovery Channel, and believed that all things were ultimately explainable by science. Still, he could not help but wonder, if the amulet actually did possess special powers, what form would they take? How would they prevent him from cheating?

Donny looked at the ground then, and was surprised to see his wife below him. She smiled up at him, a pair of scissors in one hand, the amulet at her feet.

Cut it loose, the medicine woman had said. *Cut it loose and let it fall.*

HERBERT'S FIRST JOB
by John Moran

I was resting in Hell when the portal appeared.

"We need a type one demon," shouted the thing in charge of logistics.

A little later, he added, "Type twos. Get here now." A minute after that, "Type threes—anyone?"

I tugged the edge of his wing.

"They're in Asia Minor fighting in the wizard war."

"All of them?"

"Yes."

"So what am I supposed to do? We can't ignore a summons."

"Send me."

"What the heaven are you?"

"Type six sprite, sir."

"Have you ever been summoned?"

"There's a first time for everything, right?"

He frowned, looked round in desperation, then shrugged and burned a glyph onto the air.

"You know the rules: fulfill your summoner's wishes to the letter, and be rewarded with power and lands. Fail, and torture will be thy lot."

"To the letter?" I said.

"That's it. Get through quickly."

* * *

I emerged into a teak-paneled hall between a pair of black candles. The ceiling was open to the stars, revealing a tall tower where a zeppelin was tethered.

I turned invisible, preparing my entrance to impress my new master.

"Spirit of Hell, I call thee," my summoner said. Dressed in a purple hat and cloak with a Toledo rapier at his waist, I knew him instinctively as Count Philippe di Courtuga, lord of the castle and its surrounding lands. Beside him stood a slimmer figure dressed as a butler.

I waited as they completed the spell.

"Hazel sticks, Vincente," the Count said.

"Yes, my lord."

"Curse the dratted woman."

"Indeed, my Lord."

"So I'm clumsy, am I? Have the courting manners of a drunken Spaniard, do I? I've had no other complaints."

"No-one would dare, my Lord."

"Damn right! Mandrake."

Vincente upended a squirming leather bag, and the root fell screaming onto the flames.

I felt the tug of compulsion, and used every appearance trick I'd learned from the big boys. Five candles lit spontaneously around the room, dust whirled in a vortex from floor to ceiling and lightning crackled like the discharge of an etheric gun.

"What," Philippe asked, "are you?"

"I'm a sprite, my Lord. My name's Herbert."

"Where's my mezzo-demon?"

This was not going well. I lifted my left foot and scratched my right ear in confusion. "There's only me available, my Lord."

Philippe snarled and thrust his rapier at me. I fled to the far edge of the magic circle.

"Begone, useless weakling," he shouted.

Had I failed already? I hung my head and began to fade.

"My Lord?" Vincente said.

"Yes?"

"That was our last mandrake."

Philippe sighed. "Wait. You'll have to do."

"Certainly master," I became solid once more. "Tell me your will."

"I demand..." Philippe paused and pushed out his

chest. "Wrath upon the Countess Montefeltro."

My forehead ached as I struggled to understand. I was only part-way through infernal studies and my grasp of human was poor.

"Wrath?"

"Ruination."

"You want me to turn her to rubble?"

"Decimate, despoil, extirpate her. Be her bane."

Philippe paused when I continued shaking my head.

"Make her miserable," he said at last.

"Ah," I said. "That I understand."

"Then go."

I rejoiced in my mission, but hadn't the slightest idea how to carry it out.

"Er. Would you mind if I wander your domain in human form first? Ask questions of the locals, that sort of thing?"

Philippe nodded.

I sped off, taking human form to mingle with his servants. When I inquired about the best way to make a woman miserable, the answer rang the same from everyone.

I returned to find Philippe striding the walls of his castle. Thunder cracked the heavens as lightning struck a tower nearby and ran along a metal strip to safety.

"I have a plan my lord, but it needs clarification."

"Proceed."

"May I do anything to make her miserable?"

"Of course. The more sadistic, the better."

"Do you want her to recognize you as being responsible?"

"Nothing would give me greater pleasure. Not only do I want this, I command it!"

"Then we are ready." I produced the box I'd spent the last hour crafting and revealed a dozen papers within. "These are forged, to come from Lord Gattario, a rebel with ties to the Spanish. If it is discovered in her chamber, she will be ruined politically. For full effect, you should be the one to reveal it."

"Except I am banned from her castle."

I smiled.

"I have heard that the lady is shallow and vain. If you allow me to press your advances, you will break her heart as well as her status."

"Even after I described her as a pregnant hog with stubble to match?"

"Trust me, my lord."

Philippe clapped his hands together. "Very well. Destroy her, Herbert. Whatever the cost."

I flew across the land, my spirit darkly joyous, and crept into the bed-chamber of Carlotta, fifteenth Countess of Montefeltro. Her eyes were brilliant blue, her bosom high and her waist narrow, though her legs were thick and her voice like clanging brass.

I sat watching for two hours while her maid Lisa brushed her hair.

"Do you think I'm the most beautiful person in the city?" Carlotta asked.

"Undoubtedly, Mistress."

"Do you think I'm the most beautiful in the country?"

"Few would argue."

"I think," continued the Countess, "that I'm the most beautiful in the whole world."

"You are as knowledgeable as you are beautiful, Mistress."

Because my first apparition didn't go as I'd hoped, I put some extra magic into my second. The air shimmered and the room trembled. Two china dogs fell off a shelf, the dark velvet curtains before the casement swung closed, and the multi-pronged candelabra on the black granite mantelpiece lit itself.

I appeared as a pale-skinned footman, kneeling with a bunch of flowers.

"Who are you?" the Countess said.

"I come from Philippe di Cortuga."

"That worm? I've already told him what I think."

"Indeed, lady, which is why I return with his deepest apologies. Knowing your beauty he desired to court you, but became tongue-tied in your presence."

"That's understandable."

"I bring flowers, regrets, and a petition from the depth of his sorrow that you might allow him another attempt."

The Countess sniffed. "I am known for my tolerance."

"And your ready affections," Lisa said.

The Countess stared coldly at her. "If I ever find you using humor again, I'll have you whipped." She turned back to me. "Tell your master I accept, though I don't come cheap."

I watched the maid struggle to control herself, and bowed.

"Thank you, Lady."

I vanished in a shower of rose petals, then sped through the air to find Philippe groping a maid aboard his airship. The butler stood nearby, looking discretely away.

"Did she reject you?" Philippe asked.

"Of course not, Lord. She will now allow your zeppelin within her airspace. All you have to do is plant the box and seduce her to her room."

"You're sure this will work?"

"Everyone assures me this is the perfect way to make a woman miserable."

"Excellent!" Philippe dispatched the maid with a slap on the behind, then turned to his assistant. "And while I'm sneaking, you can distract her, Vincente. It'll give you a chance to see that maid of hers again, though why you're interested in someone of low status I have no idea."

"We believe we have much in common, my Lord," Vincente said.

* * *

I had just finished my preparations when the airship cruised to a halt outside Carlotta's balcony. Philippe stepped across, placed his ear to the glass and listened. A moment later, he freed the latch with his dagger and stepped inside.

Thanks to me, the room was a riot of color. Roses covered every surface, in vases, schooners and fluted wine glasses. Pink candles burned above the fireplace, while Carlotta's four poster bed had ribbons tied to it.

The noise of a dinner party rose through the floor.

I watched Philippe creep forward and curl his lip at the decoration, unaware it was my doing. He placed the box on the mantelpiece, then stole down the staircase. It took an hour before he returned, leading Vincente, the maid, and a number of dignitaries. As I suggested, he had his fingers covering Carlotta's eyes.

"Ta da," Philippe said, dropping his hands so she could see what had been done to her room.

She clapped her hands and turned to her guests. "You see the response my beauty brings."

"But wait," Philippe said, "what's this?" He walked to the mantelpiece and picked up the box.

"Is that a present?"

"A box this beautiful has to contain something special," Philippe said. He flipped open the lid and offered it to her, then froze. Instead of the letters, I'd substituted his mother's engagement ring on a velvet pillow.

Carlotta beamed, took the ring from his twitching grasp and placed it on her finger.

"I accept," she said.

The guests applauded politely. Behind them, Vincente reached out and squeezed the maid's hand.

Six months later, I watched invisibly as double festivities ran into the night. Vincente and Lisa swore some meaningless vows before heading off to a cottage in the woods, but my heart was with Philippe and the moment of his triumph.

I watched as, breath wheezing, he attempted to carry his bride through the door to his chamber. After dropping her on the bed, he spent ten minutes in front of the mirror re-aligning his moustache. Then he moved towards her with what looked like great reluctance.

Shortly afterwards, the two of them lay on their backs and stared at the ceiling.

"You can praise me now," the Count said.

"If you think three minutes of adolescent fumbling is sufficient, you've got another thing coming," Carlotta said.

The Count stood. "You, madam, have the manners of

a baboon."

"And you make love like one."

"Well get used to it," he shouted, "because from now on I'm all you're getting."

He stormed onto the balcony, slamming the door behind him.

I appeared and waved. This was the moment all demons savor, when the mission is complete and the compulsion to obey dissipates.

"I hope you are happy, my Lord?" I said.

He screamed at me. "You made me marry that harpy!"

With this final confirmation, I bowed and vanished, though I allowed my voice to linger long enough for him to hear it after I was gone, "and I am informed by all parties, my Lord, that nothing else can make a woman so miserable."

* * *

When I returned to Hell, I reported to the thing in charge of logistics.

"That was an interesting approach," he said.

"You did say to follow his instructions to the letter."

He nodded. "And she certainly will be miserable."

I grinned. "Even more so, when the King finds the documents I placed in his palace."

The thing in charge of logistics put his wing around

me and smiled. "You know," he said, "I'm beginning to think you may be a natural."

BRAGGING RIGHTS
by Sharon Goldberg

Ever since her boyfriend Todd broke up with her, Ginger's obsession with Luke Hastings, lead singer of Yellow Fever, had crescendoed. Todd said she was clingy, needy, an energy suck. He said his time was better spent on his music. And he was sick of hearing about that drug-crazed rock star whose songs were so late seventies. Ginger was crushed and cried for days. She'd been Todd's biggest fan, attended all his performances, told everyone she met about his band, even papered cars in parking lots with flyers promoting their shows.

Screw him, her best friend Lisa said. If Todd had one ounce of the talent Luke had maybe his band would be playing the Kingdome instead of some crappy club in Kent.

Ginger cherished the t-shirt she'd purchased at Yellow Fever's Seattle concert three years ago. It was black with Luke pictured from the bellybutton up, naked, a monstrous mosquito painted on his chest, its wings extended, its eyes bulging, a puddle of blood next to its legs. Below the bug, the band's name was printed in gold Gothic letters. On the back,

"The Blood Sucker Tour 1983" dripped in red above a list of thirty-six cities including Portland, where Ginger and Lisa had driven the day after the show to see the band a second time. The t-shirt was a size large so Ginger could wear it to bed. She lay there and moaned and writhed and imagined Luke next to her, on top of her, underneath her, his fluffy chestnut hair tickling her shoulders, his pointy tongue flicking her nipples, his strong, guitar-strumming fingers weaving their way down her thighs as if he were pressing the struts of his headless Steinberger Trans Trem.

Ginger had read in *Rolling Stone* that Luke had the biggest cock in rock. He was a sex god, a supremely-skilled lover who guaranteed his women a thrilling, screaming rollercoaster ride. (Todd, although enthusiastic, was not theme-park exciting.) Two girls from Chicago called the PlasterCasters had made a mold of Luke's penis when Yellow Fever played there. They added it to their collection which included Mick Jagger, Steven Tyler, and Seattle's Jimi Hendrix. Ginger thought all the Fever members were smokin' hot, even Lance, the bass player, who supposedly penetrated a Miami groupie with a banana and, on the band's last Seattle trip, tied a girl to a hotel bed and, during foreplay, exploited a cold, whole salmon from the Pike Place Market. That did not appeal to Ginger. Luke, she hoped, was a bit more conventional.

In Portland, she and Lisa had tried to get backstage. They'd flirted with the security guy, begged him, almost snuck in with some skanky, bleached blondes, but the guard blocked their way and told them to go home or they'd be arrested. This time, Ginger was absolutely, positively determined to meet Luke, ask him to sign her new concert t-shirt, and above all, have sex with him. Her friends would be soooo jealous. And she'd prove to Todd he'd made a huge mistake breaking up with her.

She absolutely, positively had to snag a backstage pass. Not any pass. A laminated all-access pass with cool graphics hung on a lanyard. The passes were rare, doled out selectively to media, record store owners, friends, and girls who traveled with the band. Ginger decided her best option was a press pass. She found the name of the concert promotion company and called. She tried to sound professional, official, entitled.

"I'm with the Daily at the University of Washington and I'm covering the Yellow Fever concert for the paper. I'd like two press passes, please."

"Sorry," the receptionist said. "We only give out passes to the major papers and stations."

"But the school is full of Fever fans!"

"Sorry."

A half hour later, Ginger called back, lowered her voice, and said she was with KYYX radio.

"And what's your name?"

"Ginger Glick."

"Just a sec." The receptionist put Ginger on hold, then

clicked her back. "Your name isn't on their list."

"There must be some mistake."

"Talk to your general manager."

Ginger called back a third time, desperate.

"How do I get a backstage pass for Yellow Fever? Just tell me. I'll do anything."

"You have to know someone and you obviously don't." Click.

Ginger would not allow a rude, self-involved, sub-zero receptionist to get in the way of her destiny. After Todd broke up with her, she'd read "You Can Heal Your Life" by Louise Hay. She learned about affirmations and how they could change her life. She practiced hers over and over:

I will stop loving Todd.

I am intelligent and hot.

I deserve floor seats to the Fever concert.

I deserve an all access backstage pass.

I will meet Luke.

Luke and I will experience a deep connection.

I will have amazing, astonishing, mind-blowing sex with Luke.

Six weeks before the concert, tickets went on sale. Ginger camped out at the Kingdome for three days. She was number four in line and scored two floor seats in row three. She'd be close enough to see Luke sweat. Close enough to clutch Luke's hand when he strutted down the ego ramp that jutted into the audience. Close enough to dash on stage after the concert before security caught up with her. But she still needed a backstage pass. Two weeks later, KYYX announced a contest. Three times a day, listeners could call in for a chance to win VIP concert tickets. Each designated caller who correctly answered a question about Yellow Fever would be invited to the "Meet and Greet" after the show. And get their picture taken with the band. And get an autographed poster.

Yes! The affirmations were working.

On the first day of the contest, Ginger skipped classes and stayed home to call the station. When the DJ announced the contest question, she knew the answer. What was Yellow Fever's first platinum hit? Easy. "105 Degrees." She dialed the station and prayed she'd be caller number twenty-five. Busy. Redial. Busy. Redial. Busy. Redial. Ring. "You're caller number twenty-two, try again." Shit! So close. Ginger repeated the process three times a day for the next thirteen days. She knew all the answers to all the questions: Where was Luke born? Paramus, New Jersey. What was his favorite beverage? Jack Daniels on the rocks. Where was the band formed? Rutgers University when Luke was a sophomore. He'd graduated with a degree in Comparative Literature. What pet did the band travel with? A purebred Bengal cat named Kama Sutra. But Ginger was never the winning caller.

Time was running out. Ginger repeated her affirmations over and over. Phoned the Kingdome office. Pestered her Uncle who knew someone in marketing at *The*

Seattle Times. Cornered the manager of Tower Records. No luck. She spent hours watching Yellow Fever videos on MTV and played all their albums over and over and over, mesmerized by Luke's voice, memorizing his every nuance. When she and Todd started dating, he'd written a song for her called "Sweet Ginger." Every time his band played it, she felt special. She felt loved. She felt very, very cool. She missed Todd—his sleepy blue eyes, his tender attention. Maybe Luke would write a song about her—a way better song. A number one hit. A song that expressed his great depth and sensitivity. A song permeated with passion. A song that professed his un-lacquered love. She would be famous, immortalized, like "My Sharona" by The Knack.

On the Saturday night before the concert, Ginger and Lisa barhopped in Pioneer Square. Outside The Fenix, they stopped to gossip with Jordan, the bouncer, who they knew from Garfield High. He was tall and bulky with the neck of a linebacker. Ginger remembered he sometimes worked security at The Dome.

"Do you know anyone who can get me a backstage pass?" Ginger said.

"Nah," Jordan said. "But you could go to the Dome at lunchtime, before sound check, and track down one of the roadies. I heard Luke gives the crew passes to hand out to the hottest chicks. The guys initial the passes, and whichever girl Luke ends up with, her pimp gets a hundred bucks."

"Oh my God, really?" Ginger gripped Jordan's arm.

"Really. But wouldn't you rather get it on with me?"

"In your dreams." She planted a kiss on his cheek. "But thanks."

Ginger bought a new outfit for the concert inspired by Cyndi Lauper: a short, flouncy, lavender skirt, cream lace bustier, lots of bangle bracelets, and long, dangly earrings. She'd read in a *People* interview that Luke was into girls who were smart and blonde and sexy. She would impress him with her butter-yellow highlights and knowledge of literature. She'd written a paper for Contemporary American Poetry about his song lyrics. She got an "A" and an "A" in the class, too. She'd tell Luke she compared him to Bob Dylan and Edgar Allen Poe. They'd have an intellectual conversation before they had sex. Ginger gathered all her party essentials in a leather shoulder bag—perfume, deodorant, hair brush, hair spray, *tic tacs*, camera, and condoms, in case Luke ran out.

The day of the concert, Ginger parked her car on Jackson Street and traipsed three blocks to the Kingdome. She wore her tightest jeans, a poppy and white striped halter top, and white, Nine West platform sandals. In the parking lot, she scuttled past a row of 18-wheelers, their ramps down, and continued toward the stage entrance.

I deserve a backstage pass. I deserve a backstage pass. I will get a backstage pass.

She spotted a man outside the door smoking a

cigarette. He looked like a Hell's Angel: dirty jeans, Led Zeppelin t-shirt, black ponytail, and an animal fang hanging from a leather string around his neck. She sashayed up to him.

"Hi, I'm Ginger."

The roadie snickered; he was missing a front tooth. "Hey, Ginger." He dropped his cigarette on the ground and stamped it out.

She inched toward him. "I have tickets to the concert. I'm a huge, huge fan."

"I'll bet you are."

"I'm just wondering if there's any way I can get a backstage pass."

"I might could arrange that." He looked her up and down. "Wait here." He disappeared inside the Dome. Ginger felt a thrilling tingle of hope; she was close, so close. She shut her eyes and imagined the warmth of Luke's skin, the lean muscles of his arms, the calluses on his fingers.

"Wake up!" The roadie startled her. He handed her a laminated pass.

She held it as if it were The Silver Chalice. "I really, really, really appreciate this. I can't thank you enough."

"Probably not."

"Any chance I could have another one for my friend?"

"Don't push your luck."

Ginger looped the pass over her head. The initials "JP" were printed on the back in black marker. Maybe she and

JP would both get lucky.

Ginger and Lisa drove to the concert separately since Lisa wouldn't be allowed backstage. "It's okay," she told Ginger. "You're the one who's crazy-nuts-obsessed. I really hope you get in Luke's pants."

They met at their seats. Ginger had bought the souvenir program and two yolk-yellow t-shirts with black splatters and black letters announcing "Yellow Fever/Black Vomit 1986." She stuffed one shirt in her shoulder bag and gave the other to Lisa.

"You're so sweet," Lisa pulled the "T" over her teal tank top, then smoothed her long, layered, auburn hair. She smiled, flashing dimples.

The opening act, an up-and-coming band Todd admired, played a pop-rock set. The audience meandered in and out of their seats, chattered, and applauded half-heartedly. During intermission, Ginger lined up at the restroom and Lisa bought them beer and nachos. When they returned to their seats, Ginger's heart pounded like a cranked-up ghetto blaster.

The canned intermission music stopped, the Dome lights dimmed, and the stage went black. Feedback from the sound system scratched through the air. The arena fell quiet except for the hiss of whispers and a few shrill whistles. Then, as if receiving a telepathic signal, the crowd erupted and chanted Fever, Fever, Fever, Luke, Luke, Luke. Ginger shivered. Dark figures rippled across the stage making final adjustments to equipment. An announcer's voice rang out; "And now, ladies and gentlemen, Yellow Fever!"

Sixty-thousand fans screamed a single, searing note. A hideous buzzing pierced the air, the sound of a jungle full of mating insects. The lead guitar. Strobes of gold light flashed, practically blinding the audience, illuminating a monstrous metal sculpture. A mosquito. The backup guitar joined the lead, then the booming bass, then the keyboards, finally the thundering drums. From beneath the stage, a platform rose, revealing the band, everyone except Luke. From high above, like a God, Luke descended on a wire, sheathed in gold spandex pants and a black leather jacket—no shirt—fringe hanging to his knees and fringe hanging from his sleeves, his arms extended like wings, the flashing light haloing his hair. The crowd cheered even louder. Luke landed behind a microphone, center stage, gazed into the audience and sneered. He grasped the mic and growled the opening lyrics to "Inside You," Ginger's favorite Fever song.

Your eyes as deep as caverns. Your lips a wounded red.

Your body, so soft and wiiiiiiiilling. Won't you let me inside your head?

Luke caressed the mic stand and swiveled his hips and thousands of girls answered with another eardrum-shattering scream, affirming their willingness to let him go wherever he wanted. He grabbed the mic from its perch and strutted to the front of the stage. Ginger moaned. He pranced left, right, then over to the lead guitarist who harmonized on the song's chorus. When the drummer banged out his solo, Luke gestured grandly toward him and stamped his foot to the beat. As he finished the song, the lead guitar warbling with his words, Luke stretched the final syllable over one-two-three-four-five notes. He punctuated the last one by pointing his left index finger at the floor seats. Ginger was certain he was pointing right at her. Luke had singled her out, signaled her. She squealed like a piglet and hyperventilated with near hysteria.

The band played for an hour, vibrating the Dome with rocked-out anthems and penetrating power ballads, with hyperactive drum beats, subsonic bass throbs, and pulsing synth strains. Luke leaped from the drum risers, kicked like Bruce Lee, rumbled down the ramp and clasped the hands of rabid fans. Girls threw their panties on the stage—a train of nylon, silk, satin. Luke sweat buckets. Combed his hand through his long, damp hair. Sang like he might never sing again, his voice feral, fearless, shameless, howling, haunting, holy, giving it all to his fans. Ginger felt dizzy and delirious as if her temperature had spiked to one-oh-three. She believed she could see into Luke's soul.

After three encores, after the house lights blazed on, after Lisa hugged her good-bye, after the crowd filed out of the arena, Ginger waited in line at the backstage entrance with dozens of girls. All pretty. All wearing skimpy clothes. All dying to get their slimy hands on Luke. She had to find a way to shine, to prove she had class and smarts even if she was throwing herself at him.

A guy at the door checked her pass and motioned her inside. The place was already teeming with people. Ginger scanned the scene. Two bartenders opened beers and mixed drinks behind a makeshift bar. Against one wall, a buffet table was covered with deli platters, cookies, and brownies. A gaggle of girls danced to blasting heavy metal music, some with each other, some with the crew, some with random guys, maybe from The Press. Atop a round table, two blondes wearing only bras and panties wiggled and flailed and laughed. The sweet smell of pot wafted through the air. The band hadn't yet joined the party.

Ginger whispered *I deserve to be with Luke. Luke will be drawn to me like a magnet.*

A door to a side room opened and the band wandered in, Luke last, swigging from a Jack Daniels bottle. Two girls pounced on him immediately. *I'm prettier than they are*, Ginger decided.

Lance, the freaky bass player, sidled up to her and drew her close.

"Hey there," he said. "Having a good time?"

"You bet," Ginger said.

Lance stared openly at her breasts. His hand drifted down over her butt.

Ginger remembered the banana incident. "I have to find the restroom."

He licked his lips. "Hurry back."

Ginger scooted away, located the restroom, and locked the door. She peed. Touched up her make up. Sprayed Charlie cologne on her neck and wrists. *I am not a skank. I am not a slut,* she said to the mirror. *I deserve to have sex with Luke. I deserve to be his girlfriend.* She marched out of the bathroom. Bee-lined for the bar and ordered a rum and coke. Downed it and asked for another. She mingled, talked to people about the concert, chatted with some of the other girls, one who claimed to have screwed both Jon Bon Jovi and Eddie Van Halen, and waited for her opportunity. A few minutes later, Luke disengaged from a giggling groupie and headed toward the food table. Ginger threaded through the crowd and intercepted him as he picked up a brownie.

"I have to thank you, Luke." She grinned and posed as if she were on a red carpet. "I got an "A" in my Poetry class because of you.

Luke raised one thick eyebrow. "Yeah? How'd I make that happen?"

Ginger told him the story. Told him she'd analyzed his lyrics. Told him she'd compared him to Dylan and Poe.

"Edgar Allen Poe, huh? I like that."

"Yeah. He's so dark. So edgy."

Luke flashed his luscious, lusty smile. "What's your

name, angel?"

He called her angel.

"Ginger."

He motioned to a man. Was he the band manager?

"Pete, give Ginger here a key to my room."

Pete plucked a key from his pocket and handed it to her. "Olympic Hotel. Five-eighteen."

"I have some more partying to do," Luke said. "Meet me there in an hour."

"I'll be waiting." Ginger glowed like a neon sign. "Oh, Pete, would you take our picture, please?" She handed him her Minolta.

Luke wrapped his arm around her shoulder and pressed his cheek to hers. Pete snapped Ginger's victory smile.

In the hotel room, Ginger undressed completely, folded her clothes, and placed them on an arm chair. She slipped on her new t-shirt, tied the ends together in a knot just below her crotch, and waited for Luke. She felt as amped as a driver in the Indy 500. As lucky as the winner of a million dollar lottery. As special as a rainbow. Luke was even cuter in person than he was in pictures. And he was soooo sweet. So in tune with her. He was a rock star, but he was a person, too.

Ginger waited. And she waited. And she waited. 2:00 AM. Where was he already? She knew the band was leaving early in the morning to fly to San Francisco. She turned on the TV and tuned in Letterman. Flipped through the pages of a

Seattle visitor's magazine. Stared out the window at the traffic on Fourth Avenue. She tried out the king-sized bed, lay on the cranberry quilted spread, rested her head on a down pillow. She thought of ways to surprise Luke, tantalize him, blow him away. At 3:00AM, Ginger heard a click in the door and Luke staggered in, still brandishing a Jack Daniels bottle. He blinked and zigzagged over to her.

"Hi, angel." He held out the bottle. "Want some"?

"Sure." Ginger pressed the bottle that had touched Luke's lips to hers—an act of communion, a holy moment. She swallowed. Choked. Doubled over and coughed and coughed and coughed. Bourbon dripped down her t-shirt.

"You okay?" Luke clapped her on the back.

"I think so."

Luke caressed Ginger's shoulder and squinted. "That shirt lookssss good on you," he slurred.

"Would you sign it?"

"Sure." Luke listed to one side then steadied himself.

Ginger fished a magic marker from her purse. She tapped the spot over her right breast. "Here."

Luke scrawled his name, then fondled her breast.

"Mmmmm," Ginger said.

"Back at ya. Let's get nnnnaked." He struggled out of his leather jacket and dropped it on the floor. Kicked off his shoes. Plopped on the bed.

Ginger crawled across the covers as she imagined

Luke's Bengal kitty would. "Meowww," she said and licked his chest. She unzipped his spandex pants and slid them down his legs. "Would you like me to dance for you?"

"Sure, baby."

Ginger stood and straddled him. She unknotted her t-shirt and inched it over her body and head. She sang:

Your eyes as deep as caverns. Your lips a wounded red.

Your body, so soft and wiiiiiiiilling. Won't you let me inside your head?

Swirling her pelvis like a hula dancer, she snaked her hands down her thighs, then leaned forward and lifted her breasts toward Luke. She closed her eyes and opened her lips and circled them with her tongue. She turned, bent over, and wiggled her taut butt. She felt sexy. Desirable. Dirty in the best possible way. She turned back and opened her eyes.

Luke let out a loud snort. He was asleep.

Ginger snuggled down next to him. "Luuuke." He mumbled, rolled over. Snored. Ginger cuddled up to him, pressed her breasts into his back, nibbled his ear, nuzzled his neck. He swatted at her, as if she were a mosquito.

"Fuck off," he growled.

She gasped. She felt stupid. Embarrassed. Hurt. Should she leave? Maybe he just needed a little nap. She lay there for fifteen minutes. Thirty minutes. An hour. Maybe if she woke him now, he'd be horny and less drunk and call her angel again. She pressed her hand up his thigh, slipped her fingers into his briefs, and wrapped them around the biggest cock in rock. It didn't feel any bigger than Todd's. She tiptoed her fingers down its length, tickled along the ridge. Luke farted. Ginger slid her hand out. She crawled out of bed, gathered her clothes and locked herself in the bathroom. Her affirmations weren't worth shit. Luke hadn't even kissed her. She sat on the toilet seat and cried.

Ten minutes later, Ginger got dressed. She stuffed her whiskey-wet t-shirt in her purse and padded back into the bedroom. She'd tell Lisa that Luke had been incredible, her best lover ever. She'd say Luke's penis was huge and he really knew how to use it; he'd sent chills and shivers and waves of pure passion through her body. He'd told her she was beautiful and wild and insatiable, just the way he liked his women. He'd called her "angel." She'd say Luke asked for her phone number, but she honestly didn't think he'd call. That was okay. She'd never forget that night. Ever. She had the picture to prove they were together. His autograph on her t-shirt to prove it. She'd never wash the shirt because Luke's semen was on it from when she gave him a blow job. She knew Lisa would make sure Todd heard every detail.

Ginger picked up her purse, souvenir program, and backstage pass. She gazed at Luke one last time, his face buried in the pillow, his naked body splayed on the bed. *I will stop loving musicians,* she whispered. *I am intelligent and hot. I will meet....a famous actor!*

She slunk out of the room.

I <3 LESBIANS
by Gabrielle Knock

Thomas Price had a secret. He loved lesbians. He loved them of all shapes and sizes, colors and creeds. Butch or feminine, it didn't matter, he loved them all. He liked to imagine that any two girls he saw walking together were in love, and he would write stories about those imaginings. The stories would be realistic, or fantastic, set on earth, or in space, but the one thing they always had in common were lesbians.

Thomas reasoned that lesbians are awesome because if one girl is hot, and she is naked, that is erotic (artfully-like Roman nudes, of course. Thomas was no pervert) but, if you have two naked girls, that was even better and more artful. Especially when they rubbed their breasts together.

Now this was all very well and good for a hobby, but there was a problem. Thomas didn't know any lesbians. He lived in a conservative town. When a Goth girl died in his town and her friends tried to draw a chalk drawing at the high school in memory of her, the school got the police involved for vandalism, but when a pretty blonde girl died her friends lit candles all over the school, and no one raised an eyebrow at the fire hazard.

In such a town, no one could come out as gay.

That was until Sarah Palo moved into town. Sarah was a nice girl, with a wholesome upbringing. She was good at sports and liked to knit but, best of all, she was openly a lesbian, and in Thomas's grade, too!

Thomas got lucky when they were paired together for an English project.

"So… I heard you are a lesbian," Thomas hinted.

"Yeah? So?" Sarah said, ready to defend herself against typical Midwestern homophobia.

"I just wanted to let you know I think that's great," Thomas said.

"What's great?"

"That you are a lesbian."

"What? Why?"

"Because, well, don't tell anyone, but, I love gay people." Thomas paused, gauging the look on Sarah's face. "And I really support their rights. You should be able to love whoever you want, even lesbians."

"You're a weirdo, but you're cute. We should hang out." Sarah smiled.

Thomas blushed.

And so, Thomas made a lesbian friend. Life couldn't get any better. Sarah found refuge in Thomas's secretly open mind, and Thomas found what he had always dreamt of.

They hung out constantly. Sarah taught Thomas how to knit, and Thomas showed Sarah his video game skills.

This went on until one fateful day in June. They had just finished owning some noobs at Call of Duty Modern Warfare (Cod Mod) and were sitting on Thomas' red bean bag chairs catching their breath. Their gleeful smiles spoke of their success in gunning down enemies.

Sarah broke their silent reverie with a laugh, "You have something in your hair," she said, leaning over to pick a leaf out of Thomas's lank bangs, exposing ample cleavage.

"Thanks…" Thomas felt her hand brush against his face; where her hand touched, he felt hot. She was so pretty with her bold Pixie cut and skinny jeans.

"I'm really glad we are friends, Thomas."

Thomas took a deep breath. "Sarah," he said, "I love you…" He had practiced so many times in the mirror, and yet now his words were slow in coming. "I think it is fate that, you moved to this town, and that we were partnered for English, and that you are a lesbian. I love lesbians. We were meant to be together."

Sarah stood up. "What are you talking about?"

"I love you."

"I'm a lesbian."

"I know."

"That means I like girls."

"I know, and I am prepared to deal with that. It's okay if you want to be with girls too, as long as you let me join." Thomas delighted at the thought of four breasts rubbing together just for him.

"I like girls. I don't like boys. You are a boy. What part of lesbian don't you understand?"

"I don't see gender. I don't judge you for being a lesbian. It is only the soul that matters. I love your soul, and that of all of your people."

"You bigot. Even if I did like boys, I wouldn't want you. I'm leaving."

Sarah never spoke to Thomas again.

Thomas, heartbroken, retreated back into his dreams, waiting silently for the day when a real lesbian would accept his love.

BONE OF CONTENTION
by Eric M. Bosarge

No one thought much of the pollution. Not until the dog started pooping on the kitchen table.

"What the hell?" Seth yelled.

The Pomeranian's beady eyes snapped in Seth's direction. Seeing she was caught, she pinched off the mini-loaf and skittered, claws scratching, to the edge of the table. She jumped and missed the chair, landed with a thud and a yelp.

Four feet was quite a fall for an eight-inch tall dog.

Seth walked around the table and looked down in horror. The dog, her name was Bitsy, spun in a circle on her dust-mop side, front feet scratching at the hardwood floor. Dried streaks of rust-red sediment from the ditch that had hardened in her fur flaked off on the linoleum floor.

Allison appeared in the door to the kitchen. "Oh my god! What the hell is a matter with you?" she yelled at Seth.

Lately, Seth had contemplated the notion that Allison had a secret super power: she could make him completely insane just by opening her mouth.

He instantly forgot his concern for the welfare of the dog. "Me? She shat on the table! Hello!"

The dog cried, clawed at the ground and did another one-eighty.

"But you can't yell at her! She gets scared," Allison said.

"Of course I can! Look at that!" He pointed at the steaming pile of poop on the oak table. "A healthy dog doesn't do that! That's not normal!"

"It's your fault!" she yelled.

"Mine? Mine?! Mine?!!" Seth gasped for words. Apparently, Allison could also render him completely inarticulate.

Allison's mouth twisted in a sneer. She scooped up Bitsy. "And look at her," she said, the little puff ball cradled against her boob. "Just look at her. She's hurt, baby. She needs to go to the doctor. Yes she does. She needs a *doctah-octah*."

Seth thought, she's nuts, but the way she held the pollution-poisoned, bat-shit crazy dog against her breasts still drove him mad. He took a deep breath and tried to assess the situation.

It was her fault.

"You shouldn't have let her go into the ditch. I told you not to let her go in the ditch. That water isn't safe," Seth said.

Allison ignored him. "Baby I'm so *sowwy-awwy-awwy*.

You're my *wittle* girl, yes you are. Does this hurt, baby?"
Allison touched Bitsy's leg. Bitsy pulled it back with a
whimper.

Seth pictured the dog with a bright pink cast on her
front leg, tapping her way into the putrid ditch as Allison
yelled useless, unpracticed commands at it. Of course Bitsy
would get sick again. The dog only understood gut impulses
and no matter how they begged her, Bitsy only did what Bitsy
wanted to do.

Something had to give.

As usual, it was Seth.

"You know what, I'm sorry, too," Seth said. He came
forward and rubbed Bitsy behind the ear.

Allison huffed at Seth and turned away. "Come on
baby, let's go get you cleaned up."

As Allison walked away, Seth wondered if it was time
to hang it up. This could be the final straw. He thought about
how much money he had in his bank account and calculated
how long it would take him to save a first month's rent and
security deposit.

Maybe it wasn't that bad. Maybe it would get better.
They could make it work.

He didn't think much about the pollution until later.

Allison was washing the grime from the ditch off Bitsy
when Seth joined her in the bathroom. Hair falling like a veil
in front of her face did not conceal her smile as she turned and

flicked water in Seth's direction. She tucked the hair behind her ears. Dimpled cheeks, slate gray eyes.

Seth smiled.

"Will you call the vet, baby?" Allison asked.

"I'll call the vet," Seth said.

Three-hundred twelve dollars and an x-ray later, Seth wasn't smiling. "What? No broken bones? No, fissures or cancer or…" Seth's voice trailed off.

Allison rocked the little puff dog in her arms like a baby. The dog's beady black eyes stared at Seth.

"She seems perfectly fine," the aging veterinarian said as he tucked the newly developed x-ray into a folder.

Seth thought about the poop on the table, where they *ate*, and shook his head. "She pooped on the table, doc. There's got to be something wrong."

The veterinarian shook his head. Seth told him about the ditch and the fetid red water.

"Well, I wouldn't let her go into the water if it's polluted."

"You wouldn't—" Seth took a deep breath, counting to three before he blew up, a technique he'd learned from dealing with Allison's super power. "Do you think she's brain damaged?"

The veterinarian looked at Bitsy. She licked her lips.

"You know, I really couldn't say." The veterinarian turned away from Allison and whispered conspiratorially,

"She's not the brightest to begin with. Little tiny brain." His head bobbed.

"Thanks, doc. I feel much better."

The veterinarian clapped a hand on Seth's shoulder and motioned to the door. "Don't mention it."

Allison stood up and said, "She's not stupid," as she passed the veterinarian.

The veterinarian shrugged at Seth. "It's your dog."

Later that night, Allison took Bitsy for a walk to cool down after an argument. Seth sat on the porch, eating a microwave dinner, trying to remember how the argument started. It had something to do with not paying attention to car maintenance and tire pressure. That had led to cleaning, *somehow*, or a lack of cleaning or, you only clean this, and I'm always doing this.

Then there was the toothpaste cap. The toothpaste cap was always off. Seth admitted he was guilty of that. In the mornings he wasn't awake until he had four cups of coffee, even though at night he didn't need the stuff to stay awake, so the toothpaste cap was absolutely the least of his concern at six a.m. That, the time of six a.m., had somehow led to all the many different ways they each spent money—he on his cigarettes and she on clothes and earrings and perfume and shoes. She had more shoes than any woman could wear, which was not unremarkable but Seth, being rendered temporarily insane, focused on the monetary value of said shoes and made the near-fatal mistake of bringing up the fact that she didn't work as much as he did.

She said she couldn't work that much because of her class load.

And, well, they were both in school. In fact, Seth was taking more classes than she was *and* working more.

That last thought made Seth infinitely sad. He'd thought of money because he was thinking about leaving.

He needed her financially, to continue with school. At least until he graduated. His job at Ciabatta Bread certainly couldn't pay the rent. He could live in an efficiency but, really? An efficiency? Who wants to live in one of those? What kind of girl would come to an efficiency to get down in the living/kitchen/dining/bedroom?

Allison came back up the street. Bitsy pranced along beside her, short legs a blur, until she stopped to sniff. Oblivious, Allison kept walking. Bitsy's retractable leash lengthened, lengthened, lengthened, caught. Bitsy's front feet lifted and her little body did a complete one-eighty. Tiny legs resumed their brisk walk, fairly running to keep up with Allison.

Seth shook his head.

Across the street, the neighbor hailed.

The neighbor was a thirty-something divorcee, a female divorcee, that clearly had a thing for Allison. When Seth had brought it up in the past, Allison giggled and twirled her hair. "Really? You think so?"

Allison stopped, leaned against the log fence and crossed her legs. Allison had a great ass.

Seth felt something stir in his loins and cursed Allison's super power.

Seth smiled at the thought of a three-way. He smiled more at the possibility that Allison would leave him. If she just left him it would make the decision so much easier. He wouldn't have a choice. Something shifted in his stomach and he felt sick.

Allison tossed her hair and looked back at the house. She noticed Seth sitting on the porch. The smile disappeared as she straightened and looked away quickly.

Wait, Seth thought, *where's Bitsy?*

The leash was all the way out and Bitsy was in the ditch, her puff coat flattened to her skin by the red water. She looked like a Chihuahua with bat ears.

"Damn it!" Seth shouted. Apparently, Allison's super power had rubbed off on Bitsy.

Allison jerked the leash and Bitsy flew out of the ditch like a fish on a line.

The neighbor's eyes bulged and rolled away from Allison.

Seth picked up Bitsy. He couldn't let Allison abuse her that way. She was a dog; of course she crawled into the ditch if you let her. She rolled in shit and dead bugs like perfume. You had to protect her from herself and her two year-old impulses.

"Oh!" Allison shrieked. She dropped the leash. Hands flew to her face. "Did I hurt her?"

Seth was about to bite back but held his tongue, exhaling the waste of breath. His shirt was already wet and rust-stained. He looked down at Bitsy and stroked her. A leaf was caught in the long hair behind her ear. He tugged on it and the bitch snapped. Bit Seth's hand between thumb and index finger. Seth pulled away and nearly dropped her. The pain was sharp. Rust-red water mixed with blood on his palm and in the punctures.

He grew dizzy. He wiped at the blood but the rust color just smeared into the pulsing holes Bitsy had left.

Seth imagined the pollution flowing deeper and deeper through his veins. He wondered if he'd catch a buzz, if he could market the substance to the masses and make millions, or if it would only kill him.

"Oh my god," Allison said as she inspected the cut. Seth eyed her carefully. He'd never seen her look so closely at something before. She took him by the bleeding hand and led him inside to the bathroom. She put Bitsy in the tub and closed the sliding glass door.

Seth felt very lightheaded. He wasn't sure if it was from the cut or the pollution in the water. It must have been the pollution.

Allison sat Seth down on the toilet and dabbed at the

cut with a washcloth.

Bitsy's barking sounded like sneakers squeaking on a basketball court, only sharper. She kept leaping, trying to get out of the tub, paws scraping and rattling the glass, leaving smears of red. Seth wondered how he could ever get clean in there again.

His head pounded. He could feel his pulse in his temples. He listed to one side, scrunched the toilet paper roll. He looked up at Allison and thought; I cannot defeat your super power.

"I need to fix this," Seth said.

"I know baby, I'm getting some peroxide," Allison said.

Bitsy barked her head off in the shower, angry that she was missing something.

"No. This. Us. We need to fix this or I can't do it anymore."

"Bitsy, shut up!" Allison turned back to Seth but Bitsy kept on barking. "I'm sorry, what? I couldn't hear you."

The glass door shifted a little. Bitsy nosed it open and she was out, dancing around the bathroom in celebration, barking, shouting at them to pay attention to her. She stopped and licked Seth's pant leg, her foxy little ears pinned back as her tongue worked away.

Allison said, "Aww! She's saying she's sorry, baby!"

Allison held Seth and they watched. Her arms around

him and her chest against his face felt good.

Bitsy stopped licking, ran to the center of the bathroom, put her front and back paws together and took a shit.

WALTER AND GABRIELLA
by Catherine Austin Alexander

Gabriella arrives home from the library with an armful of books. She plops down in the recliner and leafs through the first one–a volume of poems by Pablo Neruda—and there it is, between two middle pages, a $500 bill. On the front of the bill, President McKinley glares at her, as if asking, "What the hell am I doing in a poetry book?"

Gabriella hasn't had $500 to herself, much less in one bill, since her husband Walter lost his job three months ago.

The bill looks new, but a little limp. "Must be fake," she thinks.

"Not fake," says the teller at Banner Bank. "Although these big bills have not been printed since 1969, they're still in circulation."

Why was the money in the book? Could Neruda have put it there before he died, and Gabriella is the first to discover it? Perhaps he was sending her a message. Crazy, but who knows?

What should she do? Return the bill and the book to the library? How would they handle the money? Contact the previous borrower?

She decides to return the book by its due date, without the bill.

Should she tell her husband?

Later, maybe.

Nevertheless, Gabriella starts planning about ways to spend the money—that lapis and silver pendant she's wanted for so long. It'd be something just for her. The other half of the money she'd spend on Walter.

No, that wouldn't be right. Bills must be paid and the rent for the house is going up first of the year.

Better put the money away for a while. But where? In the desk? Under the mattress? On the top shelf of the closet? Maybe the garage. No, Walter would surely find it there.

So, Gabriella finally decides to slip the bill under her panties in her underwear drawer. She'll think about it later.

But she can't stop thinking about it *now*.

At the dining room table, Walter has fallen asleep on top of the crossword puzzle he's been trying to finish. She tiptoes around the kitchen while making dinner.

* * *

Walter and Gabriella tied the knot two years ago. She's not entirely satisfied with Walter—hanging around the house makes him cranky. But jobs are few. He spends his time solving crossword puzzles, reading men's magazines and sleeping. Doesn't talk much. They rarely have sex. Wouldn't it be fun to tell him she found a $500 bill that hasn't been printed since 1969? But Gabriella knows she must keep it a secret. For how long? She doesn't know.

Luckily, her temporary job at the medical center has become permanent. Sadly, she doesn't much like the work. She's a medical records clerk, under the watchful eye of a nasty supervisor. Worse yet, Gabriella must dodge the abuse of doctors, nurses, staff and patients if she can't locate a file immediately. Every week she pours through the hospital's job openings. One day she'll get out of this damn department. One day Walter will find a job. In the meantime, when she gets really down, she pictures that money in her underwear drawer.

Then one day it isn't there. She throws all her panties out of the drawer. What she is looking for has evaporated. There's no bill. No $500.

Who would take it?

There is only one person who could: Walter.

Gabriella decides to confront him, *now*.

But Walter is asleep at the table.

"Walter, wake up. I need to ask you something."

He lifts his head, wipes off the drool from his chin and blinks his eyes.

"Walter!"

"Huh?"

"I need to talk to you."

"About what?"

"Something in my drawer."

"What drawer?"

"Where I keep my underwear."

"What about it?"

"There was something under my panties."

"Under your panties?"

"Yes. Did you find it?"

"Find what?"

"What was under my panties."

"If I knew what it was, I'd tell you. But I never go in your underwear drawer to find whatever is apparently missing."

"Walter!"

"What?"

"You are the only other person in this house. No one else could have gone into my underwear drawer and looked under my stack of panties."

"Maybe you just thought you put this item under your panties. Maybe you put this item somewhere else and forgot about it."

"I did not put this 'item', as you call it, somewhere else."

"If you could let me know what you've lost, perhaps I

can help you find it."

"Does President McKinley ring a bell?"

"Sure. William McKinley was assassinated in 1901. That means he couldn't have gotten into your panties. Theodore Roosevelt succeeded him."

"Walter!"

"What?"

"Please stop. You know perfectly well what I'm talking about."

"I do?"

"You're a liar."

"I'm going upstairs, Gabriella. I've lost my appetite."

The next morning the $500 bill is back under Gabriella's panties in her underwear drawer.

"Walter!"

"What?"

"Don't give me that *what*."

"Okay. I took one of your panties."

"You did what?"

"Now you're giving me that *what*."

"Just explain, Walter."

"All right. Come sit down on the bed and I'll try to explain. This won't be easy."

"I'm all ears, Walter."

"Well, you know the men's magazines I like. In one of them, there's this picture of a guy wearing girls' panties. It just sort of turned me on."

"Turned you on?"

"Exactly. So I borrowed a pair of yours and walked around the house wearing them. You know, admiring myself in the mirror."

"Admiring yourself in *my* panties?"

"That's not so bad. Some guys like sniffing girls' panties."

"Christ all mighty. And that explains why the item was stolen?"

"You mean the money?"

"What else would I be talking about?"

"Okay, I took it. Went to Banner Bank and they told me a lady was there just yesterday with one exactly like it. I asked the teller if it was real and it is."

"Then what did you plan on doing with it?"

"I really wanted to buy you that lapis and silver pendant you've been admiring in the window at Sterling's. The rest of the money, well I didn't have any plans for it. But when you confronted me about something missing in your drawer, I decided to return the money."

"How thoughtful of you."

"May I ask, Gabriella, where did *you* find the money?

"Wait a minute and I'll show you."

She rushes downstairs for Neruda's book and brings it back.

"It was in this volume I got from the library. After the page with the poem called 'Absence,' believe it or not. Right here, see? I'm not kidding!"

"Wait a minute. You're telling me that you found the $500 bill here?"

"It's the God's truth."

"Did you think to return the bill to the library?"

"For about a minute."

"Okay, then, let's spend it!" You're going have that piece of jewelry today. I want to see you wearing it."

"Hold on, Walter. You have some explaining to do. What is this business of parading around in my underpants?"

"It's just fun. Perhaps I'm a bit of a cross-dresser. No big deal."

"A cross-dresser?"

"Doesn't mean anything, Gabriella. Would you like to see me in your underpants?"

"Absolutely not, that's disgusting. Get away from me. How could you ever suggest such a thing? You think you look good in my panties?"

"Like to see?"

"Never! Well...maybe just for a minute."

Walter quickly slips into a frilly nylon pair.

Gabriella stands back to evaluate. "Well, actually you look kinda sexy."

"I do? Well, come over here."

"Ooh, Walter, such soft panties. Ooh."

"You like? Pat me a little more."

"Walter, does this mean we'll be having sex again?"

"What do you think?"

"No more whats, okay?"

"Okay. It's a deal. Now how 'bout trying to get into my panties?"

"Watch out, here I come."

"Oh, this is so fine, Walter honey. And just think, we have Neruda to thank. We're $500 richer and have our sex life back."

"Yeah, wonderful."

"You don't sound too thrilled."

"I am, but..."

"But what?"

"Wish I had a job."

"Walter!"

"What?"

"I got an idea. You know that nightclub downtown called "Gusty Winds?" It's a drag queen place. Bet you could make big money. Even have a new career!"

Walter scratches his head. "There's a thought. But I don't know. Sounds crazy."

"Why?"

"Is it legal?"

"Of course it's legal," says Gabriella, laughing. "And

you look so cute in panties. You'll be a smash."

"You think?"

"I'm positive."

"Suppose I could try it. Better than sitting around doing crossword puzzles."

"Now you're talking, honey. You're gonna go from crosswords to cross-dressing!

"C'mon upstairs, Walter baby, and try on some of my fishnet stockings."

RED STARBUCKS GIRL
by Lisa Douglass

I guess you just come right out and say it like it is. Right? That's what I was thinking, eating my burnt toast. The sunlight shone on our little breakfast nook and the scene looked warm, like two people had made a home together. Two people that liked each other and enjoyed conversation that didn't make the other want to take an ice pick and shove it deep into that part right above the eye.

"I don't love you anymore," I said, expecting a reaction but Catherine was doing her makeup in the bedroom.

"That's nice, darling," Catherine said.

It had come to this. Walls between us. Paper mâché cats instead of real ones. Secret mold in the bathroom that we smelled but couldn't see.

"I had sex with a dog once. Not real sex, more like I put peanut butter on my balls," I said.

"You can tell me about it after lunch, dear," Catherine said.

I was not Catherine's first choice, in fact she told me once that my dick was only a third of the size of her last boyfriend, but that this shouldn't discourage me, she liked my mind.

"His dick was smaller the second time, that's all I know," she said when pressed. "The first time I thought it was at least fourteen inches."

I was doing the division in my head thinking a third of fourteen means close to five, right? In a world where division makes a kind of sense that stops me from eating a mess of pills—Catherine must have meant that the previous dick, the dick that belonged to the guy she would not name but simply called "Monkey"—that dick had to be more like fifteen inches to make mine feel like five.

"I measured it, and it was seven inches and sometimes eight," I heard myself say, but I couldn't remember if it were true. I opened the junk drawer looking for a tape measure and a magazine I had hidden away, called *Jugs*. I went to the bathroom to check it all out. To make it hard and then measure it. But, I got too excited and came before I could do it proper. It looked so big, I turned myself on too much, like when I stared into Catherine's asshole and would have to explain why that made me come.

The problem with Catherine was she the best-looking girl I'd ever known. I knew someday she'd leave me and everyday I was with her, I tried to get back at her for it. It made it hard to get close.

"Why do you think we look so young, Catherine?"

"Maybe all the drugs, from when we were stupid," Catherine says.

"Maybe…" I said.

"How old do I look?" Catherine said. I looked at her up and down.

"You look a solid forty," I said.

"What?"

"That's a compliment…like a cougar is a compliment."

"Fuck you."

I had been in love with someone else at the time. Mostly, to help myself not be so attached to Catherine. Catherine was the type that got free drinks at Starbucks and everyone gathered around her wherever she went—to be honest, I was jealous.

The girl I fake-loved was Red Starbucks Girl. That was the name I had given her. Red Starbucks Girl, because she always had something red with her. Red scarf or lipstick or shoes. Something red.

Red Starbucks girl couldn't look me in the eye. She would fidget with her fingers when she saw me, making letters in the air like my grandmother used to do on my back.

"Guess what it is?" my grandmother would say.

"B?" I'd guess.

"No, try again."

"R?" I tried.

"No. Now, pay attention, Pauly, I don't have all day."

She did it again, there were three parts to the letter as far as I could tell.

"H?" I guessed.

"That's a good boy," my grandmother said.

Red Starbucks Girl's eyes were far apart like a Down's Syndromed girl I was forced to play with in childhood. I considered she may or may not have been making signs to me with her air-gestures. I watched her so much as to creep myself out, but couldn't help it. She tried to look away from me but her eyes would just kind of go everywhere, not ever resting. I wondered if she knew my cock was more like eight or nine inches instead of fourteen. I even wondered if she had ever had a fourteen-inch cock inside of her and how that even works.

Red Starbucks Girl had something wrong with her, and that was what made me love her. Her weird sign language was just a nervous thing she did, because there was no one there to see it—except for me and I was sitting at another table. I imagined her signing to someone she never met, but hoped to meet back in the land where she came from. I imagined she came from a land of twigs and snow and possibly a pony bought for her before she was old enough to understand that a pony was just a girl's version of cock.

Red Starbucks Girl was going to be mine. Although her gestures were to an empty space ten inches in front of her face, I parsed meaning out of them to be some kind of come on.

This type of communication was hardly anything at all, but it was better than what I had with Catherine, who had stopped paying attention to anything I said. That was my fault. I was always going to leave, but never did. Plus, I loved her in a way; on the days where I actually thought love was something you could do or give to a person. The rest of the time, I felt bored.

Anyway, in Red Starbucks Girl's mind I must have done something to her, victimized her in some way that she wasn't going to talk about. I made up stories about how she was writing in her little red book about me and how I had slighted her. It must have been something other than fuck her in the bathroom of *Susina Bakery* next door saying things like:

"Do you like that, you little fucking whore?"

She grunted.

"That's right, you slut," I said shoving myself inside of her. I pulled her hair to really get her going.

"Stop pulling my hair, that hurts," Red Starbucks Girl said, slapping my hand away and then punching me on top of my head with knuckles and everything.

I stopped talking altogether then. I was afraid I'd make her mad. Then she said,

"Why'd you stop saying weird stuff?"

"I want to tie you up," I said, not knowing if that was in fact part of the "weird stuff." It was so hard to know.

She just kept fucking me, so I guessed I was doing okay. And really that was it. She got off and then I got off after it was clear she already had.

"I'm sorry," I said.

"What a weird thing to say. Why would you say that?"

"I just came so much," I said. "It's been a while."

"Tell that nonsense to someone else," she said as she cleaned herself up in the sink.

"You go out first," she said.

I did like I was told and then she came out and we both went back next door and resumed our spots at Starbucks pretending not to know each other.

The next day after I got to Starbucks to do my writing I said, "Hey there," because I didn't know her name.

"Hi," Red Starbucks Girl said without really looking at me. So, that means she didn't want to talk, so I walked away in a state of rejection although I tried to cover it by joking with the baristas about a pair of breasts I had seen earlier.

"They were like cartoons, these ones were."

"What does that even mean?" my barista friend, Lester said.

I looked back at Red to see if she were listening, but she was talking animatedly to a guy with a fake tan and that stuff you comb into your hair to make you look younger. I hated that fake tan guy. He made me want to kill something.

I tried to think of what it was like before. Did she ever

look at me then? Or was she always like this? Over the next few weeks we grew further apart. It was clear she did not want to know me.

Then, one day she slipped me a note and we went back over to the bakery and she got on her knees and gave me a blowjob.

"You like that in your mouth, you whore. You slut. You like my big cock?"

She put her hand up to shush me.

"Stop saying that. What are you, twelve?" she said.

So, I shut up then and stared at the Moroccan tiles and the fake antique holder of the toilet paper and let her do her business. I told myself she was retarded.

After that interaction, things got worse.

I'd see her and she'd say, Hi Pauly, then look away as if I had embarrassed her somehow by having my cock in her mouth. I didn't know why she was so cold. I mean, she really had seemed to like my cock, so what was going on?

She was so weird that I thought maybe I had done something besides fuck her. My mind could not understand where she had gone. But, really, had she ever been there at all? I had turned into a girl, that was the one clear thing. This was what girls did with their circular logic about a guy after sex.

One day, maybe two weeks later, but in guy time it might have only been a day, I just have no idea, she told me, "You have a girlfriend."

"It's not what you think," I said. "I'm in great conflict about the girlfriend." I didn't even sit down. She wasn't asking me to. She was giving it to me with her eyes.

"Don't you care how you're hurting your girlfriend?"

"I'm not hurting anybody. She doesn't even like me anymore."

She waited a long time, surveying my face, but I was a great blank.

"That's not what worries me," she said. "It's the way you justify your loose morality with such conviction. This is why we will never be in love."

She went back to her work. I was standing there saying, "But…"

This conversation was over, she never turned back to look at me and we never spoke about it again.

Back at home with Catherine was the same. I'd say weird stuff hoping she would fight for the relationship, but she wouldn't bite. I thought that meant she didn't love me.

One morning she was making coffee. I sat on the couch playing Avengers Alliance with my friends on Facebook.

"Do you like this outfit?" Catherine said.

"Want the truth or a lie?" I said.

"The truth," Catherine said.

"You look old and I don't know if a change of clothes will help that."

Catherine just stared at me. I never had seen her crack

and wasn't thinking she would now.

"You left your gmail open," Catherine said. "If you want to talk about it we can, but I think if you want to sleep with another girl you should just move out."

"Yeah. We're in love with one another."

"You always think it's love, but still. I can't have someone around who's mean anymore. Dog licking your balls or whatever you're into."

"It was only the once or twice."

Catherine left the room and changed her outfit and went out without saying goodbye. She was wearing something bright this time, as if bright could change her age, but I didn't mean it. She was the most beautiful woman I knew. I don't know why I said it. Guess for the sake of winning. It felt good in a way. Now, I could be alone and eat Hot Pockets whenever I wanted to.

FISH STORY
by Payne Ratner

I'm at my desk at work and a fish falls in my lap. It's greasy with water and still flexes. Still alive. The gills pump open and shut.

It twists its head and looks at me and says, Did I make it?

It's so utterly shocking that I'm simply not shocked. I look at it. Watch it begin to die.

Maybe my heart is going a bit fast. I can't tell.

There's a damp gray, soggy spot in the ceiling panel overhead. No hole. Just a bit of a sag.

So then I think, okay, someone's being funny. Some ventriloquist chucked a fish from a rubber bag over the wall of my cubicle. I stand up, look, but no one's looking.

Ha ha, I think, ha fricking ha.

But first things first. This fish needs water.

I don't know if it's fresh or salt, but wet I know for sure will help.

The men's room is right across from me. I take the fish in and plop it in the toilet. It's too big but at least I get its head and gills in the water so it can breathe.

I stop up the sink and turn on the tap.

What I'll do is get it revived a bit then run it down to the fountain by the Italian restaurant until I can get it to a lake or a pet store.

But this isn't really a pet.

It's an ugly, broke-jawed, mean looking thing that's scared silly, I bet.

The sink is full and I hear this clap, clap. This weak slap of its tail against the sides of the toilet. I lift it by the tail and ease it in the sink water. It's pretty limp but the sink is too small for it to turn its belly up so I think that's a good thing. If its belly can't go up it can't die.

I think, I'm spending more time on this fish than I have on my marriage in five years.

Mitch Wardenstone comes in.

Whatcha got there? he says.

He leans over so I smell his lunch.

It's a fish, he says.

He goes into the stall, sits down. Waits for a second. Then he comes out.

I don't know why I went in there, he said.

Then he goes to the urinal and stands there for five minutes while I watch the fish twitch a little and its gills work half-way.

He's back there and he's not pissing.

Oh, well, he says.

He zips up and comes over.

It's this goddamn medication, he says.

He looks in the sink.

How'm I gonna wash my hands, he says.

You can use the kitchenette, I say, the little sink in there.

Oh, yeah.

He takes hold of the handle.

See you at the meeting, he says.

Oh, shit, I say, when's it start, again?

Like, he says. He looks at his watch. Like now.

Shit, I say, I still need to print that shit.

It's not printed?

I was going to now but this.

I look at the fish. It looks a little better but the drain doesn't hold and the sink is half empty.

Can you watch this thing, I say.

The fish?

Like, two minutes.

What's it gonna help to watch it?

Just give it a little water when it starts to run out.

Okay, but hurry.

I go out, pull up the document, hit print, go back in.

The water's almost gone. The fish has a panicked look on its face. Mitch is standing in front of the urinal. I turn on the tap.

I gotta talk to this asshole doctor of mine, Mitch says.

He zips up.

Still nothing, he says. But the urge. It's like Hoover Dam, he says.

Tell them I'll be there in a second, I say.

I look down and the fish gives me this pathetic don't-ever-leave-me-look and I know I'm sunk.

* * *

What're you doing home, my wife says.

Her boyfriend comes in behind her. Carl. All shoulders and neck.

Hi, Carl, I say.

Hi, Tom.

I kinda got a situation at work, I say.

What kinda situation, she says.

I'm gonna take a shower, Carl says.

The mail? She says.

Oh, yeah.

He hands her a stack of bills and glossy ads, drops his coat on the Lazy Boy and goes off to the bathroom.

The guy takes more showers than a rain forest, my wife says.

He's self-conscious about his glands, I say.

That's all psychological, she says.

But things ooze out of him, I say, tropical oils.

That's a load of crap, she says, he's a sloppy eater, period.

Why d'you stay with him, I say.

You don't want to know, she says.

I do.

My mom's new boyfriend, Tom the shrink, says if it wasn't for him I'd be too afraid to stay with you. He says Carl's 'cause I love you so much.

Great way to show it, I say.

I know, I'm sorry, it's just, you know, I don't know, whatever.

Why's he say I put up with it? I say.

He can't figure that out, she says.

She sits on the sofa, pops off her shoe with her toe.

Oh, God, what a day, she says. Lady was allergic to one of the perfumes. I sprayed one puff and she went down like I'd shot her through the head. We had to call EMT.

Is she okay?

Yes, but discolored. She looks like a sunset. What's your situation at work?

The bad news is, my situation at work is that I don't have a job, now.

My wife puts her head on the back of the sofa like she's been hit with a hammer.

You better, my wife says, be mother-fucking kidding.

I guess there was some straw somewhere that broke

some camel's back, I say.

What the fuck are we gonna do, she says, what in the fucking hell?

I know, I say, I'm sorry.

You know what the landlord said, she says.

I know, I know.

And Carl. Is gonna be so pissed.

Do we have to tell him tonight?

No, she says, we don't. And not because I'm a nice guy. Because the reason is, I want to rip your head off myself.

She bounces the back of her head against the sofa.

Fuck fuck fuck, she says.

Then she looks at me.

And how's he gonna buy his medicine? She says.

It's not medicine, I say, it's steroids. Will someone please stop calling it medicine?

Either way, she says, we are seriously fucked. And don't expect me to steal again.

I never wanted you to steal in the first place, I say.

We put our heads back and look at the ceiling. It's hard to believe that she and I ever made love. And she once put her head on my chest and listened to my heart beat.

We are so, so major-league fucked, she says.

But the good news is, I say, is, we got a fish.

Then Carl screams.

It's horrible to hear. Part high-pitched girl in a horror

movie, part stuck pig, part man with shrunk testicles.

He stands beside the bathtub with a handful of towel clutched over him. His mouth looks like a raisin.

What the hell's that?

I brought it home from work, I say.

We watch it swish its tail. It spreads some kind of milky cloud around the tub.

What's it doing, spawning? My wife says.

I don't know.

It looks good, though, I think. Happy and healthy. Glossy. Its gills pinked up. It looks like it's grown an inch or two.

Look at this, Carl says.

He sets his foot on the side of the tub. There's a small oval wound.

I think it bit me, he says.

Better wash that out, Dee says.

Can fish have rabies? Carl asks.

He stands at the sink with his leg cocked and lathers up his foot.

What'd they give that for? Like a turkey or something? A ham or something?

It just fell in my lap, I say.

Why didn't you take, like, movie passes, something not so slimy?

It wasn't like a gift they gave me.

What about an iTouch? What's wrong with an iTouch?

Nothing.

Guy at the gym has an iTouch.

Is he gay, I say.

Carl gives me a look.

By ten o'clock Carl's a fish, too.

* * *

Dee sits on the toilet and watches them. The two fish circle around and rub each other. The bathroom develops this odor.

It was so weird, Dee says. He was brushing his teeth, then he got this look like something kicked him in the back of the head and then it was like the air going out of a balloon. He went flying all round the room and then plopped in the water. Then there was all this splashing. Next thing you know, there he is.

I look down.

I never seen a fish with blue eyes, I say.

Watch when he swims this way, she says.

Oh, my God, I say.

You see the abs?

Jesus, I say.

The bath water explodes and this thing flies out at me. I knock it down on the floor. It lands like a piece of thick, heavy, wet, living rubber that works itself this way and that.

Fucker tried to get me, I say, fucker went for my throat.

He is one pissed fish, Dee says.

She picks him up. He pours out of her hand into the water. Then he turns and glares at me.

If I were you, she said, I would not use this toilet.

I'm going in the kitchen sink, I say.

I would too, she says, and you know how I feel about germs.

You know something, I say, that's the nicest thing you said to me in a long time.

* * *

The moon has lit the fuses of all the cats. They're all screaming in pain. One or two pop like firecrackers.

I get off the sofa and go in and look at Dee asleep in bed. As quiet and slow as I can I climb under the sheets, careful not to touch her. I lean on my elbow and watch her breathe.

She opens her eyes and looks at me.

What?

I was thinking, I say, that what if this fish has come to bring us together?

How, she says.

I don't know, I say, stranger things have happened.

Not that strange, she says.

Then she turns her back to me and slowly falls asleep. I stay on the edge all night and think about her body. And fish swimming inside of her.

I ease myself over and whisper in her ear, What about we have a baby?

* * *

In the morning I get up, get my old baseball bat from the closet and go in the bathroom. She stands there with her hands across her belly and looks in the tub. I have my bat ready in case I gotta pop it outta the air.

They seem bigger, she says.

They do, I say.

Then the one with Carl's eyes thrashes once and actually puts its head out of the water and stares at me and snaps its gills open and shut. Its face actually gets a little red. Then it slips backward into the water.

The other fish just watches. Cool and silver. With a little silver smile on its face. Like it's got everything under control. Like it's enjoying the show.

What're we gonna feed them?

Fish food, I guess, I say.

You got money, she says.

No. You?

No.

What for food? Like we have bread or something? Something they'd like?

We have that frozen wedding cake, she said.

I thought about that cake, huddled in the corner of the empty freezer, spikes of frost all over it, like the quills of a frightened porcupine. I thought of that day, so full of light and hope.

I don't know, I say, maybe something else.

It'd probably poison them, she said.

I guess, I said.

A jar of salsa.

What do fish eat, anyway?

Fuck, she says, maybe I have to steal.

You are not gonna steal.

I take her by the elbow, I turn her around to look me in the eye.

Do not steal. You want to go to jail? Go to a meeting, I say, but you are not gonna steal. Okay? Promise me.

We gonna let Carl starve?

Just promise me, okay?

I hold her arms. I look at her.

Okay, she says, Jesus, I promise. But what about Hilda?

Hilda, I say, who's Hilda?

That's what I named your fish.

How d'you know it's a girl?

You just do, she says.

Hilda turns, looks up at me. If fish could have long eyelashes, she would. And for a fish, full lips.

I see what you mean, I say.

Dee looks down into the water. She bites white marks in her bottom lip.

Are you jealous? I say.

I'm starving, she says.

* * *

After she goes to work I lie on the sofa and watch the spot where the TV used to be. We pawned it last month for food, which was a mistake. Pastor Wallchist said, Man shall not live by bread alone.

At noon the landlord comes by. He knocks hard.

In case anyone's in there, he yells, which I know there is, I'm coming by with the police on Thursday. I got all the legal papers here. I'm sliding 'em under here. For your reading pleasure.

I hear the hiss and crinkle of a fat envelope forced under the door.

I get up, go in the bathroom. The fish are barely moving, like they've been listening.

I turn on the water to get it fresh.

Carl seems less angry. More thoughtful. Hilda has a serious expression on her face. They both bob up to the surface and look at me.

It's okay, I say, there's nothing to worry about.

But you can see they're both worried.

* * *

Dee looks half deflated when she gets home.

You and your fucking promise, she says. We coulda had some buffalo wings and peanuts and some food for the fish but whenever I tried to pick up a little something for us it was like a dog bit me. It wasn't a promise it was a fucking curse.

She peels her sleeve back, there's red marks all over her hand.

I'm sorry, I say, but next time they said was jail.

Three hots and a cot, she says, doesn't seem too bad at the present moment. How's the fish?

I don't know, I fell asleep.

We go in, look at them.

They look depressed, she says.

The landlord came by, I say.

And?

Day after tomorrow.

Dee looks back at the fishes.

You think he'll ever turn back, she says.

That depends, I say, if you love him. Do you love him?

Dee looks back at Carl. He eyes her. He curls his body left, then right, like he was flexing up his biceps. Hilda watches him. She rolls her eyes and turns away.

Dee bursts into tears.

I'm sorry, baby, she says, I'm so sorry.

Are you talking to him or me, I say.

Leave me alone, she says, all of you.

* * *

That night for dinner we sit at the table and flip through Gourmet magazine.

Oh, God, Dee says each time we turn a page.

Oh, my god, she says, oh, yeah.

I lay my hand across a sweaty lamb chop.

You're getting me all stirred up, I say.

Get your hand off that chop, she says.

Remember what Pastor Wallchist said, Man shall not live by bread alone.

Just then there's a ruckus in the bathroom. We run in. The water swirls and bucks. Inside the tub the fish have gone from silver scales to a kind of brown. There's a film of water on the floor. Carl launches himself out of the tub, lands on the floor and starts to wriggle towards the door. Then Hilda leaps out and lands in front of him. She squiggles around and slaps him twice across the face. Then she flops around and stares him in the eye. For awhile their mouths flap open and shut, like they're having an argument in a language we can't hear. Then Carl gets this look in his eyes and limps up and falls over on his side. His gills work pretty hard. Dee picks up Carl and I pick up Hilda and we slip them back in the water.

* * *

That night I ease into bed while Dee's asleep and lick my fingertip and touch her nipple and watch her face. I think, somehow, I touched the on switch for a dream. I remove my hand and put it in my pocket.

In the morning she says, I can't get up.

Why?

I had a dream.

What kind of dream.

A dream dream, stupid. What other kind is there.

The dream paralyzed you?

How about I haven't eaten in four days? That have anything to do with it?

Boy, you are one serious grouch.

Why can't you have a mother and a father we can mooch off of for awhile? Jesus. What good are you?

Can you tell me what your dream was?

That everything's gonna work out.

And that's why you're upset?

Do you ever listen to anything I say, she said.

I go in the bathroom, check on the fish. They're, like, weaving together. Like, making a braid of water if you could braid water.

Hi guys, I say, how's it going?

But they ignore me.

I go back in.

How are they?

They're acting very strange.

Will you do me a favor, Dee says, will you go look under the green picnic bench in the park and bring back what you find?

Are you serious?

Yes.

And see if you can borrow a phone and tell them I'm not coming in to work.

Today?

Today and maybe tomorrow and maybe not.

Not, what?

She stops talking and nothing I can say will get her started.

* * *

It takes me a long time to find the right green bench. They're all green. I hope I found what she wanted. It's a grease spotted paper bag with a Morton's salt and pepper shaker inside and a lemon.

I get back and she's sitting on the kitchen counter. She looks up.

Her cheeks are red as roosters.

I had a long talk with Carl, she says.

And?

And I think, all his life he's wanted to do something good and strong and courageous but he never knew how. He thought being strong was all about having muscles.

She rubs her eye with the heel of her hand.

Anyway, she says, I think he's ready.

You think?

I don't exactly understand fish, asshole.

Boy, I said.

Think you better talk to Hilda?

Yes.

I go in. She has a hard time staying straight in the water. Carl is facing the corner of the tub.

I lift Hilda out and hold her against my chest. The cold wet slime goes straight to skin and my heart bumps up a beat.

I don't know who you are, I said, or why. But for some reason you've given me something I can't ever understand.

And then I start to cry. I have no idea why. The tears pop on the water. It's so unusual for me to cry. And to cry so much the tears actually leave my face and hit other parts of the world. Very unusual.

I carry Hilda into the kitchen. Dee hands me a knife.

I'll get Carl, she says.

I lay Hilda on the cutting board. She looks me straight in my eye and I can tell everything is happening as it should.

Dee comes in and lays Carl on the counter. She takes her mother's old hatchet.

She lifts the hatchet, I position the knife.

I feel, I say, like I'm cutting off my thumb.

* * *

We eat without a word. We eat 'til we're full. The electricity's shut off half-way through dinner but we got the light of a stubby storm candle and the bright sparks of a lemon. When we're done Dee goes into the kitchen and comes out with our old wedding cake. It's still cold, and it's lost a lot of sweet but, still, it's edible.

ABOUT THE EDITOR

Eric M. Bosarge lives and writes in Durham, Maine with his wife, Megan, and dog, Scruffy. He has an MFA in Creative Writing from the University of Southern Maine and teaches at Central Maine Community College. You can find out more about him and read more funny stories at www.erics-hysterics.com.